THE 1950s ADVENTURES OF PETE AND CAROL ANN

4

Wild Winter

CHRISTMAS, CLUES, AND CROOKS

C.A. Hart-

Hawk Prints
HENDERSON, NV

The 1950s Adventures of Pete and Carol Ann
Wild Winter: Christmas, Clues, and Crooks
Copyright ©2012 by C.A. Hartnell

Hawk Prints Publishing
Henderson, Nevada
www.hawkprintspublishing.com

Front cover illustration by Larry Ruppert
Back cover and interior illustrations by Scott Carter/Stith Printing Inc.
Graphic design by Aaron and Michelle Grayum / www.thegrayumbrella.com
and Cindy Kiple
Author photo by Jim Dorsey

Editorial team:
Cathy Griffith; Becky Barnes; Brenda Kay Coulter, Senior Editor

Good Humor-Breyers trademarks used with permission.
Scripture quoted from the King James Version of the Holy Bible.

Manufactured in the United States of America.

Houdini Printing and Publishing
Las Vegas, NV 98118
USA
www.houdiniprinting.com

September 2012

www.cahartnell.com
www.hawksride.com

ISBN 978-0-9855433-4-1

This book is dedicated to my dad, Harry James Hartnell.
During my childhood, he really did sing "The Christmas Song"
like Nat King Cole, and he still does.
Plus, he always picked out the perfect Christmas tree.
Merry Christmas, Dad.

Contents

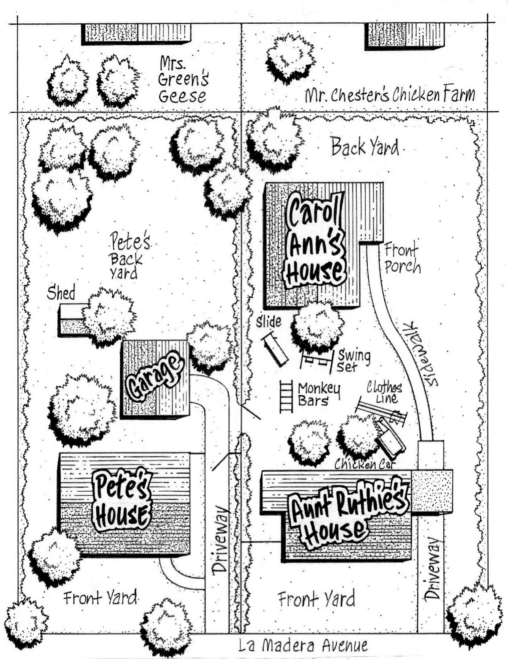

Map of Carol Ann's Yard

LIST OF CHARACTERS

THE HARTNELLS:
Carol Ann, age 11
Kathleen, age 9 (Younger Sister)
Gail, age 7 (Youngest Sister)
Mark (Baby Brother)
Jeanne (Mom)
Harry (Dad)
Granny Mary (Harry and Ruth's Mom)

THE McCAMMONS:
Dr. Ruth (Aunt Ruthie)
Dr. Charles (Uncle Charlie)
Little Charlie, age 7 (Cousin)
Cathie, age 6 (Cousin)
Jimmie (Baby Cousin)

THE HAWKINGS:
Pete, age 11
John/Hawk, age 16 (Older Brother/Owner of 1937 Ford named Hawk's Ride)
Mary Jane, age 12/13 (Older Sister)
Mandy, age 7 (Younger Sister)
Pete's Mom

HAWK'S FRIENDS:
Ernie, age 16 (Owner of 1932 Ford hot rod named Wild Panther)
Tim, age 16 (Polio Survivor)

CHICAGO RELATIVES:
Granny Catherine Biehl (Jeanne's Mom)
Great Aunt Julie Cummins (Granny Catherine's Sister)
Great Uncle Wilson Cummins (Great Aunt Julie's Husband)

NEIGHBORS:
Mr. Chester (Chicken Farmer on property behind the Hartnells)
The Cruisers and Surfers
School and Church Friends

Prologue

The songs "Dig That Crazy Santa Claus," "What Child is This?" and "It's Beginning to Look a Lot Like Christmas" played on car radios and Hi-fi stereos throughout the month of December, 1955, in El Monte, California.

The *El Monte Herald* newspaper advertised with pictures and prices of gifts, gift wrap, and groceries. A last-minute Santa could purchase a complete Christmas dinner, a battery-operated car for seventy-nine cents, towel sets, fashion jewelry, a children's story book entitled *Frosty the Snowman*, or a *Rudolf the Red-Nosed Reindeer* comic book.

Magazine covers displayed cheery Christmas scenes and pages filled with holiday cheer, advertisements, recipes, shopping hints, and seasonal stories. The holiday spirit abounded with words like giving, gifts, angels, wreaths, ribbon, greeting cards, tinsel, toys, tree toppers, sleigh rides, Santa's Village, candy canes, ornaments, jingle bells, silent night, snow, snowmen, nativity scenes, and the Christmas Story.

Passenger-filled cars cruised by brilliantly lighted Christmas scenes and decorated houses. All enjoyed the sights and sounds of the season. Baking cookies, cakes, and holiday pies spread their delicious aromas around well-stocked kitchens while children waited for tasty treats. Their Christmas stockings had been hung on fireplace mantels, doors, and walls.

Local businesses sent out season's greetings: Merry Christmas, Best Wishes, Happy Holidays, Noel, Tidings of Great Joy, and Peace on Earth. Youth groups set up workshops to fix toys for needy kids, raised money for The Community Chest, and sang Christmas carols in concerts. While "Have Yourself a Merry Little Christmas" played, certain circumstances turned Pete and Carol Ann's season of joy into a wild winter. Can they salvage the true gift of Christmas?

1
December First

Raindrops tapped on my umbrella as Pete and I shuffled on the wet sidewalk to our friend's modern-looking house. Pete pressed the doorbell, and a ringing sound echoed inside Stu's home. A Christmas wreath with a red bow adorned his front door. Ceramic elves posed on snowy white, sparkly felt arranged across a ledge inside the picture window. Soon, footsteps hurried in our direction, and the door opened.

"Merry Christmas, Pete and Carol Ann," said Stu as he stepped out onto his porch. "I'm leaving, Mom!" he called back inside his house then closed the door.

"Gee . . . Merry Christmas to you," said Pete. "But . . . isn't it too early to be saying that?"

Stu smiled and said, "December is 'Merry Christmas' month starting today."

I pulled my red raincoat hood over my brown hair, popped open my plaid umbrella, and strode into the rain. "Merry Christmas to both of you. Let's hurry up, so we're not late for school," I said as my red rain boots splashed through the sidewalk puddles.

Both boys charged off of the porch while pulling their raincoat hoods up over their heads. They splashed through a pathway of puddles while laughing, dodging, and kicking water at each other until they soaked their jeans with dark shades of wet.

Pete stopped to catch his breath and said, "Hey Stu, that's a *cool* Christmas wreath on your front door. My mom won't let us decorate our house until next week."

"My mom said the same thing," I said as we scurried like wet rats up La Madera Avenue to Cherrylee School. The walnut trees that lined both sides of our street waved their bare branches against a gray, cloud-filled sky.

Pete asked, "Have you ever thought about how many poor people live in our town? Is there anything *we* can do to give them a Merry Christmas?"

"That's so cool of you to think of them, Pete," I said. "Giving to others is what Christmas is all about. You're really hip . . . you're with it."

"He's 'with it' all right," said Stu as raindrops dripped off his nose like a face fountain.

"God gave us baby Jesus in the manger 'cause we needed him. So shouldn't we give to others in need?" answered Pete.

Raindrops tapped on my umbrella as I said, "We could earn money to give to the poor by having bake sales."

"Bake sales, yum," said Pete. "We could bake cookies and be the taste testers."

"Our moms could bake lots of goodies for us to sell," I said. "What else could we do?"

Stu said, "A fundraiser-type gig would be fun and would raise lots of money. We could do a Christmas play and invite people from all over town."

Pete piped up, "What about putting on a play with a parade and charge admission."

We turned the corner onto the street called The Wye that led to Cherrylee School. The Wye split into two different streets that curved around our school like a horseshoe. Leafless, winter trees surrounded the Art Deco buildings.

"I think Stu's idea of putting on a play would be a blast," I said.

"We could be like the actor Mickey Rooney in one of his movies where he puts on a play. Our teacher wants us to write a play or story about Christmas. I'll write a play with animals . . . like the ones that might have been in the stable when Jesus was born."

"That might work as long as I can hide in a costume, make noises, and don't have to say any lines," Pete said then turned toward the rumbling sound behind him.

VROOM, VROOM. Hawk's Ride, a cool 1937 Ford two-door Sedan with a slantback and chopped top, roared up next to us. Pete's brother had cut the car's top off, chopped down the window walls, then welded the top back on. The car's seventeen-year-old driver and owner, John "Hawk" Hawking, rolled down his window to talk to eleven-year-old Pete.

"Hey, Pete, did you get your lunch money?" asked Hawk.

"I got the bread . . . the money . . . Mom left me to buy lunch," said Pete.

"No sweat," said Pete's brother. "Have a boss day at school, Kids." As Hawk pulled away, we heard the song, "Santa Claus is Coming to Town," blaring from the car's radio.

Hawk popped the clutch in his red-orange, chrome-plated machine and punched it. Gold-painted flames on the car's sides sparkled in the rain. The hot rod cut out up the street on its way to El Monte High School where Hawk and his friends were juniors.

"Your brother is so *cool,* and so is his car. And Santa Claus *is* coming to town," said Stu as we walked onto the school grounds near the office.

"He sure is coming to town," said Pete. "And we're going to help him when we figure out a way to earn enough money to give it to needy families."

Our neighbor, Mr. Chester, stood in front of the door to the Cherrylee School Office with a group of visitors. Mr. Chester leaned on a crutch to help balance him on his legs crippled from childhood polio. A yellow rain slicker kept his overalls dry.

"Hello, Mr. Chester. It's nice to see you," I said with a smile.

"Hello, Kids," he answered. Then he said to his companions, "Follow me, so your kids can get registered." The dark-haired, dark-skinned family filed into the office behind Mr. Chester.

"That boy looks like he's our age," said Pete. "Maybe he's in our class."

Once inside our classroom, we hung up our belongings on a row of hooks along the wall. *It's Christmas in our room,* I thought. Winter and Christmas scenes adorned both bulletin boards. White, paper snowflakes circled the room next to the ceiling.

"I love the Christmas decorations Mrs. Rose put up," I said as I went to my desk. Pete and Stu scooted past me to their desks near the rear wall. I looked back at Pete and saw him sit down then get out his books and prized pencil collection box.

The school bell rang with a shrill sound. The entire class sat up straight and faced forward. Mrs. Rose departed her desk for the blackboard. Her high heels clicked across the floor. She turned to the blackboard and wrote December 1, 1955. I noticed the design detail on the back of her gray jacket and the ruffled collar of her white, silk blouse.

She turned around with a smile on her face and said, "Good morning, Students. Please stand and let's salute our flag by saying 'The Pledge of Allegiance.'"

We stood, turned to the American flag hanging on the flagpole in the corner, placed our hands over our hearts, and recited the pledge. "I pledge allegiance to the flag of the United States of America and to the republic for which it stands, one nation under God, indivisible, with liberty and justice for all." *I love saying the flag salute.*

Thirty-five chairs scraped the floor as thirty-five sixth-graders sat back down at their desks. I dug out my history book and found the right page. A small dog in one of the pictures looked like Buddy, my year-old beagle hound. *What's Buddy doing right now? I hope he's being a good doggy for Mom . . . or I'm in trouble. Yikes.*

Our classroom door opened to reveal the school secretary and the dark-haired boy we saw with Mr. Chester. The new boy stood straight and tall as he looked across our sea of faces. I smiled at him, and he smiled back. I heard whispers behind me.

"He's so dark, different . . . colored." I glanced back to see Angela straighten up after whispering to Edith and Neil. All eyes looked at the doorway . . . at the new boy.

Mrs. Rose said, "Let's all welcome Adam."

"Welcome to our class, Adam," we said in one voice.

Our teacher smiled at Adam and said, "Please tell us your full name, where you're from, and where you live now."

Speaking with confidence, Adam said, "My name is Adam Stiles. My family moved to El Monte, California, from Alabama."

"Thank you, Adam," said Mrs. Rose. "There's an empty desk next to Mr. Hawking. I'm sure he'll be happy to show you around as he's our 'student in the know.'"

"Righto," said Pete motioning Adam in his direction. "I'll show him around."

Pete nodded to Adam as the new boy sat down at the desk next to him. To my surprise, Pete even offered him one of his precious pencils. Then we went back to work on our history lesson. Some time later, the lunch bell rang with a shrill ringing sound.

Books slammed shut, and papers rustled as we prepared to split for the cafetorium. My stomach growled in anticipation . . . spaghetti with meatballs, garlic bread, salad, and chocolate cake. *Yum. No sandwich with chips and cookies wrapped in wax paper and nestled in my Dale Evans lunch pail. Today, I get to buy my lunch. Double yum!*

Mrs. Rose dismissed us. I grabbed my raincoat and followed Edith out the door. I noticed her shabby raincoat and worn-out boots. *I feel sorry for Edith. Even though she's poor, at least she gets to go to a great school, to learn, and to make friends.*

Pete and his friends headed for the door, but Adam stayed back. Pete noticed, so he circled over to Adam and said, "You're welcome to eat lunch with us. Where's your lunch pail? I have extra lunch money if you need it."

"Thanks," said Adam. "My mom forgot to give me some."

Bob Bailey ran ahead of us under the overhanging roofline and yelled, "Last one in the door is a rotten egg."

We raced forward and crowded around the cafetorium door to get in first and not be rotten. The rain pounded on the roof like a drum, cascaded in miniature waterfalls along the roof edge, then dented the grass and dirt along the walkway.

Once inside the crowded cafetorium, I stood in line behind the boys. The smell of spaghetti sauce wafted through the huge room competing with the wet puppy smell of so many wet . . . pupils. One day last spring, Pete and his friends had acted so wild that I had expected them to swing like monkeys from the uniquely carved rafters above us.

Today, wild kids hurried around us, but Pete stayed in line next to Adam. We paid for our food, found an empty table, then sat down to eat and talk with our new friend. Like Edith, Adam's clothes looked clean but shabby. *How many kids have money problems?*

After lunch, we filed back to our classroom. The rainy day kept us inside rather than outside on the playground for games of Marbles, Jump Rope, Foursquare, Tether Ball, or Hopscotch. I stopped at the drinking fountain, but I didn't take a drink. I wrinkled my nose at the big glob of pink, gooey gum getting ready to dribble down in pink strings from the spout. *Yuk.*

In our classroom, I sat with a group of kids that included Adam. During our lunch break, we aimed questions at Adam. They flew at the new boy like friendly arrows. He courteously answered everyone. Mrs. Rose looked up from where she sat at her desk and smiled. I smiled back.

Pete pointed at the row of windows with rain splattering against them and whispered, "That's some wild weather out there. Is this the beginning of a wild winter?"

"I hope we don't have the wild weather we had last October," I said. "We barely escaped from two cloudbursts and a dangerous dust devil."

"Don't forget the lightning strike," said Pete.

When the school bell screamed, we scampered to our own desks as the rest of our class flowed into the room like a flood. Heat blowing out of the vents ruffled the paper snowflakes taped around the edge of the ceiling.

We worked on our schoolwork for the next few hours until the final bell rang shrilly. Everyone slapped books closed, shuffled papers, and waited to cut out of the classroom like a fleet of hot rods at the drag races.

Mrs. Rose held up a hand and said, "Remember to study for tomorrow's math quiz and work on your writing assignments. Your short plays or stories must be turned in by Friday, December ninth. That's next Friday. Class dismissed."

Out on The Wye, our group of friends dashed through the drizzle. My raincoat, boots, and umbrella protected me from the worst of the weather. Unfortunately, the space between the bottom of my skirt and the top of my boots left my legs exposed to the chilly air.

We turned the corner onto La Madera Avenue as the Bailey brothers traveled past us like twin water spouts out in the ocean except this was the rainy road to our homes. Susan, Eileen, and

Becky waved good-bye as they sprinted in a different direction under their bobbing umbrellas.

Adam said, "I don't know how to get to Mr. Chester's place from here."

"You've got it made in the shade . . . I mean the rain," said Pete. "I'll show you how to cut through Carol Ann's backyard to Mr. Chester's yard."

"Thanks," said Adam. "And thanks for welcoming me to your school. Lots of kids would have stayed away from me 'cause, like that girl said, 'I am different.'"

"I'm sorry you heard her," I said. "She's bad news."

"Yeah," said Stu. "She's loud, and nosy, and not very nice."

"Forget her," said Pete. "What are we doing for our homework assignments? I'm writing a short story about giving to poor people in our community."

As we moved along, Adam said, "I'm writing about the new start that my family is getting here in El Monte, California, thanks to Mr. Chester."

Stu said, "I'm writing about my brother and what it's like for him to spend Christmas away from our family. Neil said he's writing about his old friend Rex and how much he misses him now that he no longer lives in El Monte."

"I'm writing a play about the animals in the stable with baby Jesus and what they can give him for a gift," I said. "But I've gotta think of a cool name for my play . . . which could be a fundraiser."

"Let's do a parade and a pageant fundraiser," said Stu, "with your play."

"Yeah," said Pete, "We can build a stage in my backyard and charge admission."

"What if the weather is gloomy and wet like today?" I asked Pete as I looked up at the cloudy sky.

"My dad sets up a tent in our backyard every Christmas for his work party," answered Pete. "We'll build a stage under the tent to protect the production."

"My dad's a carpenter," said Adam. "I'll ask him to help build the stage."

"Maybe my mom and both your moms could donate fabric and time to sew costumes, curtains, and backdrops for the stage," I volunteered.

"My dad has lumber. I'll ask him to donate some," offered Stu. "I dig these ideas. I think we're doing a Christmas pageant with lots of ticket sales to help poor people," said Stu as he veered off to his house. "See you tomorrow. Merry Christmas."

"See ya later, alligator," said Pete with a wave.

We passed Pete's house and driveway where Hawk's Ride sat with its sparkling paint job. Then we ducked into my yard. We darted past Aunt Ruthie's house on the front of our property, down the driveway, past the chicken car, past my house, and right up to the back fence.

My one-year-old doggy, named Buddy, scampered up to us and shook all over like an eggbeater. His black ears swung on his white and tan head. Buddy wiggled his black back, wagged his white-tipped tail, and looked up at us. Adam stooped down and patted him.

"Hi, doggy," said Adam. "What's your name?"

"His name is Buddy," I said. "He's a beagle hound. He loves treats and pats on the head. Buddy's first birthday is Christmas day."

Pete showed Adam the place in the fence where he could peel it back and squeeze through. "Make sure you always put the fence back so Mr. Chester's dogs don't escape."

"I will, and thanks for everything," said Adam as he ducked through the opening and put the fence back into place. He waved to us from behind the bush-covered fence while Mr. Chester's mangy, junkyard mutts barked at him. Buddy barked back.

Pete said, "Maybe Dan at Dan's Diner will let us have bake sales there in his parking lot."

I said, "We'll ask our moms to donate baked goods."

"You'd better start writing the play for our pageant," said Pete.

"I'll start it tonight," I said. "Hey, I saw you offer Adam one of your special pencils. That was very 'giving' of you."

"I'm glad he took it while he had the chance," said Pete. "During lunch, someone stole my pencils and the case. There's a crook in our class!"

"Yikes," I said. "That's bad news, Pete. I'm really sorry."

Buddy howled like he felt sorry for Pete and his missing pencils.

"Get out your little, red, spiral-sided notepad, Carol Ann," said Pete. "You can write down clues then we'll catch the crook."

"I will do that," I said as I patted the notepad in my pocket.

Pete shifted from the porch to the drizzle. He pulled up his hood and waved goodbye. "See ya later, alligator, and don't forget to ask your mom if you can go with us to Santa's Village."

"After while, crocodile, and I'll ask Mom," I called after him then ducked into my warm and welcoming home.

Wow! I hope Mom lets me go to Santa's Village with Pete and his family. Because of this rain, there should be lots of snow up there. Pete's a good friend to invite me, I thought and then frowned. *Someone isn't Pete's friend. They took his pencils. What else will they take?*

2

Santa's Village and the Cool Christmas Coat

A fist, like a sledgehammer, pounded on the bathroom door. My nine-year-old sister yelled, "Mommy, Carol Ann's hogging the bathroom again! She's hiding in her Christmas coat that Granny Catherine made for her. She doesn't like it."

I yanked open the door, strolled out, and said in a patient voice, "The bathroom's all yours, Kathleen. Don't have a cow, and I'm not hiding. I like my new coat."

I stood in the hall dressed in my warm winter clothes for snowy Santa's Village. Mom, Kathleen, baby Mark, and seven-year-old Gail gathered around me and stared. *Why are they staring? Do I look goofy in my Christmas coat? It is the brightest blue I've ever seen!*

Mom smiled and said, "You look like a movie star in the sweater coat your grandmother knitted for you. Model it for us. It's lovely, and you look lovely in it."

I turned and felt the hem of the calf-length Christmas coat flare out around me. I touched the knitted collar with the white angora edging. Then I ran my fingers down a few of the eight royal-blue, rhinestone buttons that fastened the front of the sweater coat.

Gail said, "I like that white, fuzzy, angry stuff on the cuffs and down the front."

"It's called *angora*," said Kathleen who corrected Gail's choice of words. "Carol Ann cried when she opened it 'cause her coat's not red."

Mom said, "Well, there are lots of red coats because red's a Christmas color. But there's only one special, blue sweater coat for our special girl. I wish my mother had knitted one for me when I was your age."

I felt my face frown, so I smiled instead as Mom and the kids admired my coat. *Granny Catherine was supposed to knit me a red sweater coat. Instead she made it royal-blue! It's not special to me, and I don't feel special in it! But I do feel bratty,* I thought as I tucked the money Mom handed me into my angora-trimmed pocket.

"Thanks, Mom," I said. "Pete said we'll be back after dark."

"You're welcome, Carol Ann," answered Mom. "Have fun today at Santa's Village, and remember that a gift finds value in a grateful heart."

At the front door, I stepped past my two cousins who lived in the house in front of us. Seven-year-old Little Charlie and five-year-old Cathie stared at me. *I knew it. I do look goofy in my bright-blue sweater coat.* Behind me, I heard the little kids talking.

From the porch, Gail said, "Mommy, can we go to Santy's Villager?"

Little Charlie asked, "Can I go, and can I have a blue coat, too?"

I shuffled slowly up the sidewalk that connected our house to Aunt Ruthie's house and crossed the grass next to the chicken car with its *peep, peep, cluck, cluck* sounds. Mr. Chester's chickens lived in the old, broken-down car in our yard. One of his hens scurried out of my way as if to say, "What's this big, blue goofy thing?"

Pete waved to me from the gate between our yards and said, "Hurry up, Carol Ann. Hawk's Ride is fired up and ready to cut out for snow-filled Santa's Village." He stared at me in a funny way as I walked towards him.

"What's wrong, Pete? Did I grow antlers or something?" I asked.

Pete laughed as we moved up the driveway. "I was staring at your boss threads. I like your cool Christmas coat. Did your granny in Illinois knit it for you?" he asked.

"It's the one," I said as we ducked into the back of Hawk's car. "It was supposed to be *red* . . . not *bright* blue. It's not what I had pictured in my mind."

"You don't sound very grateful," said Pete as we settled on the seat.

"Mom said that," I answered. "I feel . . . embarrassed to wear it."

Just then, Pete's thirteen-year-old sister, Mary Jane, scooted onto the backseat of the car with seven-year-old Mandy. *Why can't I have a cute, pink, store-bought outfit like Mary Jane's instead of a bright-blue, handmade sweater coat? I'm jealous.*

Mary Jane's blonde ringlets cascaded around her face as she turned to look at me. She smirked and said, "Did someone just say they were embarrassed? I would be, too, if I had to wear homemade stuff. Oh, dear, was that you, Carol Ann?"

"Yeah, Sis, and I think Carol Ann's coat is cool and unique," said Pete.

"It certainly is unique," agreed Mary Jane. "Thankfully, there's only one of them." Mary Jane smoothed out the white, fake fur trim on her pink snow jacket.

Thankfully, Hawk's Ride roared, *VROOM, VROOM,* and split for Santa's Village in the snow-covered San Bernardino Mountains. Pete's mom and Hawk's friend, Tim, sat up front. The rest of us sat squished together on the back seat like four Twinkies in a clear cellophane package.

"Hold on to your snow hats," said Hawk. "We're on our way to a fun day."

The song, "Jingle Bells," jingled out of the car's radio on the dashboard. We sang "jingle all the way" as Hawk's Ride rumbled out of the neighborhood.

Mary Jane pushed her little sister into me and once more looked at my sweater coat. "What's with the bright blue, really long sweater anyway?" she asked. "This is supposed to be a play day at Santa's Village . . . not a circus parade."

Mrs. Hawking looked back over the seat and gave Mary Jane "the look." Then she said, "I wish I had the skill to knit something so beautiful for Mandy. She needs a new winter coat."

"Well, I'll stick to pink," said Mary Jane. "Pink's my favorite color."

Pete said, "Pink like a pig, oops, I mean . . . like a pretty flower."

Mary Jane glared at us as her mother cautioned them from the front seat, "That's enough, children. What would Santa think about your bickering? It's naughty, not nice."

Hawk spoke up and said, "Route 66 is gonna take us to the city of San Bernardino where we'll take Waterman Avenue up into the mountains. It becomes Highway 18 and will lead us to Santa's Village in Skyforest."

We relaxed on the back seat of the car and listened to one Christmas song after another on the radio. Once past San Bernardino, Hawk floored it as he cruised up the mountainside. Frigid air and pine scent flowed in through the open window.

High in the mountains, white, sparkly snow covered everything. Four-foot high snowdrifts looked like giant marshmallow lumps bordering the snow-plowed road. A sign pointed one way to Lake Arrowhead and straight ahead to Skyforest. Bing Crosby sang "White Christmas" on the radio.

Hawk turned left into the Santa's Village parking lot and parked. We piled out of Hawk's Ride onto the crunchy, white snow that glistened like diamonds. My boots sank almost to my jeans peeking out from under the hem of my coat.

Hawk said, "We made the scene. Now, let's have fun in the snow."

"It's about time," complained Mary Jane as she adjusted her fake fur hat.

"*Think fast*, Carol Ann," said Pete as he grabbed a handful of snow, molded it with his gloved hands, and lobbed a snowball in my direction. *Whooossshhh.*

"I'm thinking we should get to the Welcome House as fast as we can," I said and ducked as another cold glob of white whizzed past my ear.

"Carol Ann's right. Let's split for the Welcome House," said Hawk as he helped Tim with his crutches. Tim struggled to walk on the snow with his polio-crippled legs. But like a good friend, Hawk stayed beside him.

The Santa's Village Welcome House was a long, snow-covered, log building. A giant candy cane sign stood next to the A-frame entrance. Behind the building, snow-dusted pine trees loomed up into the cloudless, blue sky. A breeze caused the trees to brush together dropping snowy bundles from their sagging boughs. Crashing sounds echoed from the forest.

Inside the entrance, we waited in line while Pete's mom paid for our passes. I fingered the money in my pocket. One of the pixies who worked at Santa's Village smiled at me. *Is she smiling at my coat because it's funny? I'm embarrassed and bratty for being ungrateful.*

We waited to go through the turnstile. Several ladies and a girl my age, all wearing full-length, chocolate-brown, mink coats, exited through the turnstile across from us.

The red-headed lady holding the girl's hand turned my way. I whispered to Pete, "Wow! That's Lucille Ball, from the "I Love Lucy" TV show. Is that her daughter? I wish my coat was mink like hers instead of this homemade one from my granny."

Lucille Ball and the girl stared at me in my royal-blue coat with white angora trim. The eight rhinestone buttons sparkled down the front like neon signs. They kept staring, and then the girl smiled at me before they walked away.

Mary Jane said, "Look! There's Lucille Ball in that gorgeous mink!"

Pete whispered in my ear, "I think Lucy's daughter likes your coat. She's rich, so she can wear a mink coat anytime, but only *you* have a one-of-a-kind, cool Christmas coat made with love by your granny in Chicago. Lucy's kid wants your coat!" *That's so cool if it's true,* I thought.

Freezing air brushed my face as we entered Santa's Village. "Thanks for saying that, Pete," I said as we shuffled through the snow to the North Pole sign. I opened my souvenir map and studied the red pathways that led visitors around the amusement park. Pete leaned in to take a look at my map.

Pete said, "Like crazy, like wow! This place is fat city . . . full of fun. Let's follow the red arrows that way." He pointed to Santa's Home and Santa's Miniature House.

Pete's mom took Mandy's gloved hand and said, "Let's go see Santa then we'll have lunch at the Pixie Pantry. The Antique Auto Ride is next to it. We can go there after we eat lunch."

"Okay," said Mandy. "I saw Santa last night at the store, and now I get to see where he lives. Can I ask him again for a twenty-three-inch, vinyl doll with rooted, washable hair?"

"Go for it," said Hawk as we waited in line to see inside Santa's house with its cute reindeer weathervane. Giant, concrete mushrooms decorated the snow-filled yard. A clock over the doorway told us the time in months instead of hours.

■ ■ ■

Sometime later, as we entered the Pixie Pantry, Mary Jane called out, "I've got dibs on that seat by the window."

While we munched our lunch, the conversation flew around the table like snowballs in a snowball fight. Hawk leaned over to

Tim and asked, "Did you hear the names of the two unbeaten football teams that made it to the CIF Playoffs?"

Tim swallowed a bite of sandwich and said, "I did. Riverside Poly High School is playing against Alhambra High School in the quarter-finals."

As Pete and I excused ourselves to leave, Mary Jane asked the teens, "How was the Sadie Hawkin's Dance at your school last Wednesday night?"

"It was a successful blast," said Hawk. "We sold one hundred and fifty tickets for couples."

As Pete opened the door to the outside air, Mary Jane ran up to us, "Hey, wait for me, you two ankle-biters. Let's go visit Silver Slipper Lake and Castle." We followed her across the crunchy snow.

Later, as we crossed the drawbridge out of the pink castle, the Bee Monorail cars buzzed over our heads on the way back to their hive on the other side of the fifteen-acre amusement park. "Here comes Santa Claus, here comes Santa Claus, right down Santa Claus Lane," blared out of the overhead speakers.

Pete said, "One of the times we went to the Santa Claus Lane Parade in Hollywood, we saw Gene Autry singing that song he wrote. It was cool to see him in his fancy western clothes."

"I wish I could have seen him," I said. "Since we're here, can we see the Doll House?"

Pete said, "Have a blast in the Doll House while I look at the Tin Soldier and Fire Engine. Then let's cruise on the Magic Train Ride."

Mary Jane said, "We'll meet you in a minute by the water wheel."

I tromped after Pete's sister into the Doll House. The interior overflowed with dolls and doll accessories. Every inch of space housed dolls in boxes, out of boxes, and hanging from the rafters. Painted wood shelves with carved poles and scalloped borders held an assortment of tiny, dainty dolls in fancy dresses and be-ribboned bonnets.

Mary Jane squealed with delight and said, "Oh, it's so pink in here. Mandy's got to see this. That doll over there looks like the one she wants from Santa."

We left that pink paradise and passed the pathway leading to the Chapel of The Little Shepherd. I glanced at a log-covered chapel with its tall, yellow-shingled church spire. *I bet the nativity, with Baby Jesus in the manger, is inside the chapel,* I thought. I sniffed the pine-scented air.

Pete waited for us at the Millwheel Toy Factory and Souvenir Shop. We crossed the bridge, traveled past a giant jack-in-the-box, circled the decorated Christmas tree, and turned to the Magic Train Ride. Delicious bakery smells flowed out of Mrs. Claus's Kitchen. *Yum.*

Loud noises crashed in the forest and echoed around us as snow slid off of heavy-laden branches. A cold gust of wind whipped around us, but I felt warm in my new coat. *That's one good thing about It,* I thought.

We hiked up to the pink Train Ticket Office where a pixie stamped our passes. Once on the train, we waved goodbye to the ride attendants dressed in German lederhosen.

The train's engine punched it and puffed down Storybook Lane past painted characters in scenes from *Humpty Dumpty*; *Hansel and Gretel*; *The Old Woman in the Shoe*; *Jack and Jill*; *Little Miss Muffet*; and *Little Boy Blue*.

Santa's Christmas Tree Forest swayed in the breeze that chilled our cheeks and noses. Giant, curved candy canes and lollypops stuck up out of the snow. When the train stopped back at its station, we exited our train car.

Pete said, "Let's feed the reindeer like those kids over there." I followed Pete to buy reindeer food from an elf. Pete pointed down and said, "Look at the elves' cool shoes. The toes are curled up."

Mary Jane stayed on the path as Pete and I went inside the fence around the Deer Feed Area. She called to us, "I'm not stupid enough to follow you in there like I did at Knott's Berry Farm. When I followed you into Knott's farmyard, I got a foot-full of grotty, stinky stuff. Have fun, Kiddos, and watch out for . . . *stuff.*"

Pete shrugged his shoulders as he pushed through the snow and said, "Is it our fault she gets goopy stuff all over her every time she goes on one of our adventures?"

"The goopy stuff finds her," I said with a laugh as a reindeer wearing a large rack of antlers on his head nibbled deer food off of my open palm. When my hand was empty, I wiped it on my jeans and said, "Mary Jane could always borrow elf shoes if hers get goopy."

Later, as we sat on fake, over-sized mushroom stools eating cookies from the Gingerbread Bakery, a bee car soared overhead. It flapped its wings and buzzed past its huge hive.

"That's our next destination," said Pete as he pointed to the wild, rolling roller coaster ride.

Mary Jane said, "I'm not riding on that. It will make a nest out of my blonde curls. You two have fun getting dipped up and down and all around."

"Hey, nice rhyme, Sis," said Pete. "Try to have some fun while we dip and sway."

After dipping and swaying on the Candy Cane Coaster, Pete and I found Mary Jane and talked her into riding on the Christmas Tree Ride. We sat in big, round Christmas ornaments that circled a snow-covered, decorated Christmas tree. The song, "Round and Round the Christmas Tree," played on outdoor speakers.

"That was a kick," said Pete as we climbed out of our "ornaments." "Hey, there's Mom and Mandy walking this way from the Post Office."

"I mailed a letter to Santa Claus," said Mandy. "I putted my return address on it."

Mrs. Hawking said, "That's what they said to do in the newspaper. Would you like to join us for the Animal Acts in that cute building?"

"Lead the way, Mom," said Pete. "After that, we want to ride the Candy Cane Sleigh Ride and whoosh down the Crooked Tree House slide."

Hawk and Tim waved us into the line going inside the Animal Acts building as we approached them. We cut in line and followed the teens into the warm interior where we left our heavy coats, hats, and gloves hanging on hooks along the wall.

Inside the theatre, reindeer, goats, baby burros, and ponies entertained us. The audience applauded after every act. When the show ended, we left the showroom for more outdoor adventures. Pete and I went with Mary Jane to retrieve our belongings.

Pete's sister said, "So far, I've kept my new, pink outfit from getting raunchy on one of your dirty adventures. I'm going with Mom to the gift shop. Ta-ta."

She strolled away from us with a big blob of something dark brown and gooey-looking attached to her backside. Straw stuck out of the brown stuff like yellow hair. *Yikes.*

"I don't know what Mary Jane sat in, but I bet it doesn't smell sweet," said Pete. "She's going to go ape when she discovers that . . . blob on her backside."

"That blob is bad news," I said as I looked at the empty hook where my coat had been hanging.

Pete looked at the empty hook next to his jacket and said, "Where's your coat?"

"I hung it up next to your jacket, and now it's gone!" I wailed.

Just then, one of Santa's elves hurried around the corner holding my coat and said, "I'm so sorry. I borrowed your sweater coat to analyze the knitting. It's beautiful." I breathed a hearty sigh of relief.

As we walked outside into the sunlight, Pete gave me a thumbs-up sign with his gloved hand and said, "I told you that your coat is cool. The elf liked it."

"Rudolf the Red-Nosed Reindeer" played over loud speakers as Pete and I boarded Santa's Candy Cane Sleigh Ride. Real reindeer with antlers pulled our long, candy cane-decorated sleigh through the evergreen forest. The reindeer shook their harness jingle bells in time with the song. Snow glistened in the fading sunlight. Cold air stung our faces.

After a stop in the Souvenir Shop, we met Pete's family at the North Pole. I clutched a bag loaded with puzzles and storybooks for the little kids left at home. Tim limped through the snow trampling on the dark shadow designs made by the towering pine trees. The wind pushed at his back like a helping hand.

I prayed, *Please, God, forgive me for complaining about a coat that's the wrong color when others like Tim have real problems. And thanks, God, that my coat isn't lost.*

At the exit, a Santa's Village character wearing an orange pumpkin head stopped us to say goodbye. Mandy ducked behind Pete's Mom and screamed in terror. Jack Pumpkinhead scurried one way while we scurried out into the parking lot.

Mandy looked back and said, "I don't like Jack the Pumpkin Eater Stealer." We tried not to laugh at her words.

Our group trudged through the piled-up snow to Hawk's hot rod. "Marshmallow World" played on the radio as we climbed into Hawk's car for the ride home. Mary Jane scrunched her face at us and turned away. Luckily, when she climbed into the car, only a stain remained where the hairy, brown blob used to be.

Pete yawned then said, "What a boss day at Santa's Village. Thanks, Mom." We echoed that sentiment as Hawk cut out of the parking lot.

An orange, gold, and hot pink sunset colored the western sky ahead of us. "Winter Wonderland" played on the radio. *And it is,* I thought.

Pete leaned towards me and whispered, "If you were writing a story about today, you could entitle it: 'Santa's Village and the Cool Christmas Coat.' I watched people stare at your coat all day long, because they loved it and thought it was special!"

"Thanks, Pete," I said. "If I ever write this story, I will remember your title for it."

I settled back on the car's seat and pressed my coat down. I patted my right pocket with the rest of my money in it. *What's that in my left pocket?* I reached in and pulled out a note. I opened it up and read my granny's writing in the fading light.

Dear Carol Ann, I made this sweater coat for you with lovely, soft yarn and angora detailing. I know you expected it to be red, but when I saw this beautiful blue yarn I knew it would make a special coat as beautiful as you are, sweet Granddaughter.

Love, from your Granny Catherine.

I slipped the note back into my angora accented pocket and smiled with gratitude for the special gift of Granny Catherine, good friends, a Christmas coat, and most importantly my change of heart. Mom was right. A gift finds its value in a grateful heart. *Will I always feel as grateful as I feel at this moment? Can I keep from acting bratty when I don't get my way?*

3

Cookie Creations

"What's buzzin, cuzzin?" asked Pete as he wandered into Mom's u-shaped kitchen and the heart of our home. "Cookie heaven must smell just like this kitchen."

Behind him, Stu and Adam sniffed the air like hound dogs tracking a scent. Buddy watched them through the open glass door, lifted his head, and sniffed with a snuffling noise. The little kids ushered Adam's younger sister, Annie, to a red, vinyl-covered seat at our red, Formica-topped, chrome-edged kitchen table.

Gail said, "Annie, take a knife, dig in the frosting, and spreadered it on the cutted-out cookie, and then you sprinklize it with sugar sprinklers."

I smiled and went back to work. Semi-sweet chocolate morsels dotted the dough mounds on the two trays of unbaked chocolate chip cookies I put into the oven of Mom's Wedgewood stove. Heat and baking smells radiated throughout the kitchen.

"Hi, Boys, sit down and frost cookies," I said as I put more dough mounds on a baking sheet. "Earlier, Mom baked green Spritz Wreaths she formed with her cookie press."

"I'll frost those gingerbread men and cut-out cookies," said Pete.

"You can each sample *one* cookie, or we won't have any for the bake sale this weekend at Dan's Diner," I warned all three boys with a smile.

Frank Sinatra crooned, "The Christmas Waltz," from Mom's

radio in our living room. The kids slopped frosting on the cut-out cookies then sprinkled them liberally with assorted sugars.

"Decorate those cookie trees, Pete," I said. "They look cool."

"I like sprinkling red sugar on these cookie bells," said Stu.

"The star cut-outs need yellow sugar," said Adam as he smiled at his little sister. "My mom worked at a bakery, so she volunteered to make pies, cakes, and brownies."

Pete said, "Mom and Mary Jane are making cookies and cupcakes."

The little kids left the table to go outside and play with Buddy. I surveyed the cookies that dotted every bit of counter space. The timer dinged on the stove's back-splash. With padded oven mitts, I pulled out the cookie sheets covered in golden "jewels."

"You're really cookin," said Pete. "Like a hot rod at the drag races."

From the living room, Judy Garland sang, "Have Yourself a Merry Little Christmas." The boys left the table to sample warm chocolate chip cookies fresh from the oven. They sang along with Miss Garland between bites of crisp cookies loaded with melted chocolate.

Late afternoon sun poured through the window adorned with Mom's curtains bordered in red calico ruffles. Outside on the patio, Buddy wagged his tail, circled a few times, and looked at me through the open door. He woofed at me, so I handed him his favorite doggy treat. Then I cleared the table of cookies, *goopy* frosting, and sprinkles.

Pete said, "Get your notepad, Carol Ann, and jot down some fundraising ideas."

Stu said, "Besides selling tickets to our pageant, we can earn money doing jobs for people in the neighborhood. We can wash cars, mow lawns, walk dogs, babysit, wrap presents, and clean houses."

"Those are all boss ideas," said Pete as he looked over at Buddy. "We can *wash* dogs, too." Buddy drooped his ear to the side like he was listening. Then he darted to his old, beat-up dog house and hid inside. "I guess Buddy doesn't want a bath."

"He's getting a bath on Christmas day when he turns one," I said.

"A birthday bath will be an uncool surprise for Buddy," said Pete.

Adam said, "If we're gonna put on a pageant in your backyard, Pete, we need to build a stage. Dad said he'll build one when we get the lumber."

"Yeah, we'll build a stage in the tent my dad's setting up in our backyard," said Pete as Gene Autry sang, "Rudolf The Red-Nosed Reindeer," from his Christmas album that played on our record player. Pete sang along with Mr. Autry as I made some notes.

"I have the Rudolf book. It was written by a dad for his little girl after her mother died," I said. "It's a cute story. Oops, I'm sorry I interrupted."

"That's okay," said Pete. "I have that book. We read it every Christmas. And My mom has fabric to donate for the stage curtains."

"My sweet Mom volunteered to sew them," I said. "She'll make costumes, too."

Stu said, "So can my mom. She loves to sew."

Pete glanced my way and asked, "Carol Ann, is your play done yet? It's due on December ninth. That's this Friday!"

"It's done except for a title," I said. "I'll copy it in my best handwriting to turn it in. Next week we'll read it and assign parts to the actors."

Stu said, "We have to turn in our stories and share current events from the newspaper that day, too. I'm sharing the article about The Community Chest needing more donations. The article says they feel deserted."

Adam said, "I want to share the article about the Elks handing out Christmas baskets to needy families and law enforcement officers handing out toys."

I said, "I'm sharing about Rosa Parks who lives in Montgomery,

Alabama. She was arrested on December first for not moving when a 'white' man wanted her seat on the bus," I glanced over at Adam who stared at me. "Rosa Parks is very courageous."

"You're courageous for sharing that article," said Adam with a smile.

"I'm sharing a hip article," said Pete. "It's about Little Oscar's gig at the Market Basket grocery store this Friday, December ninth, at three o'clock. He's the world's smallest chef 'cause he's only three feet, eleven inches."

Stu asked in an excited voice, "Is he bringing the Wienermobile?"

Pete answered, "Yep, he's driving his Wienermobile to El Monte, and he's giving out Oscar Meyer Wiener Whistles. I wanna get one."

"What are you going to get?" asked Mary Jane interrupting us. She stood in the opening between our living room and eating nook next to the kitchen. "Mom wanted me to wrap *all* her presents, so I split. What are you anklebiters doing? What's the story?"

"I'm gonna ask Mom to take me to see Little Oscar this Friday," said Pete. "We're baking cookies plus making plans for raising more money to help poor people."

Mary Jane eyeballed our kitchen then sat down next to Pete at the table. She turned up her nose at the plate of broken cookies that we'd been enjoying. "Well, if you're planning on doing fundraising, I want to help. I'm a boss director."

Gene Autry sang, "Here Comes Santa Claus, here comes Santa Claus, right down Santa Claus Lane," from his Christmas album. We sang along.

"That's it!" said Mary Jane excitedly. "We put on a parade and some kind of pageant under the tent that Dad sets up in our backyard. We sell tickets to the pageant and advertise it in the *El Monte Herald* newspaper."

Pete said, "Way to go, Sis. Those good sounds from Gene Autry made you think of doing a cool parade like The Santa Claus Lane Parade."

"I've never been to the Santa Claus Lane Parade," I said.

Mary Jane raised an eyebrow at me and said, "It's beautiful. The bands, the horses with riders, and the cars with movie stars move on Hollywood Boulevard between giant, lighted Christmas trees. Glowing bells and stars hang at intervals over the street. At the end of the parade, Santa Claus rides on a float and yells, 'Merry Christmas.'"

"Sounds like fun to me," said Stu as he got up to leave. "I've got homework to do, so I'd better split. Thanks for the cookies, Carol Ann."

"I'd better cut out, too," said Mary Jane as she got up to follow Stu. "Now that we've agreed that I'm running the fundraising production, I want to go home and make plans for our own Santa Parade. See ya later, Kiddos."

As she followed Stu and Adam to the front door, I noticed a giant, greasy spot on the back of her pink skirt. *Yikes.* I looked at the seat she had just vacated. A blob of smashed frosting with sprinkles frosted the cushion. Louis Armstrong sang, "Zat You, Santa Claus?"

"Mary Jane is going to be frosted . . . really angry when she finds out her skirt got frosted and sprinkled. Zat's not going to be good," I said. "What is good is that she's going to help us. Maybe she'll want to do a production like the cool movie, *Holiday Inn.*"

"I'd like to see that flick sometime" said Pete. "Sis is gonna be a screamer, as in someone who screams and not a fast car, when she discovers her frosted . . . backside. At least this latest raunchy mess smells better than the last smelly mess she sat in!"

"I hope we have a really cool bake sale this weekend . . . even if Mary Jane runs things," I said. "And I hope she likes my play and our plans."

"She will because she has no choice," said Pete. "Speaking of the play reminds me of something mysterious going on at school."

"I was thinking the same thing, but I didn't want to say anything in front of the other kids," I said. "I'm missing paper and lunch money from my school desk."

"Me too. So who's the thief in our classroom?" asked Pete. "We'd better find a safe place to hide the money that we make from the bake sale."

"I'm writing clues down," I said as I opened my red, three-by-five notepad.

"That's a good idea. See you tomorrow, December seventh," said Pete. "It's Pearl Harbor Day, 'a day that will live in infamy,' just like President Roosevelt said."

"Thanks for reminding me," I said. "We need to remember those courageous souls who died that day and throughout World War II. I'm glad Great Uncle Wilson made it home from Normandy, France, after the war."

"Your Great Uncle Wilson and Great Aunt Julie have had a lot of cool adventures over the years," said Pete as he took the broken cookies I had wrapped up for him to take home. "Hey, Mandy, let's go."

Pete found Mandy and moved with her out our front door and into a rainy drizzle that dampened the sidewalk. Gray clouds masked the sunset.

"Later gator," said Pete as he waved goodbye.

"After while," I said then ducked back into our house and out of the wild winter weather. I pushed my notepad into my pocket and thought, *Who's stealing our stuff? Can we keep our fundraising money safe if we're able to make some this weekend at our first bake sale?*

4

Bake Sale

"WOW! Look at that table full of goodies!" exclaimed the boy as he dragged his mother to our bake sale in the Dan's Diner parking lot. "I want that cupcake . . . please."

"You children have a lovely selection of baked goods, and they're so nicely displayed," said the Mom. "Your sign says you're raising money to give to the Community Chest that helps needy families in El Monte. I'd like to purchase five dollars' worth, please." Her boy smiled and gleefully rubbed his hands together.

Pete asked her, "Would you also like to buy tickets to The Cool Christmas Pageant on December twenty-third? Each ticket is one dollar, and all the money we raise goes to the Community Chest, too."

The mom smiled and said, "Here's three dollars for three tickets, please." We bagged her purchases then put the money in a metal cash box stashed under our table covered by a long, white tablecloth.

Her son chattered non-stop on the walk back to their car. The boy asked, "Do I get to see their pageant? Will that cute doggy be in it?"

I looked down at Buddy where he sat next to the tablecloth and said, "You *do* get to be in our pageant. We couldn't do it without you." He wagged his tail then popped up and followed Pete to the edge of the parking lot for a game of pitch the stick.

"Frosty the Snowman" floated out of Hawk's transistor radio

that we had borrowed early this morning. Christmas music filled the air and created a festive mood to encourage shopping at our bake sale table.

Cars and trucks drove by on Peck Road. Many drove into the nearly full diner parking lot. *I'm so happy we've had lots of customers*, I thought. *Earlier this morning, Mom drove us here in her Hudson Jet automobile loaded with our baked goods. Then she helped us decorate our table and put out all the cupcakes, cookies, pies, and cakes.*

I stared at a yummy-looking cupcake as Pete and Buddy sprinted back to the table and plopped down. Buddy panted with his pink tongue hanging out then dipped his head down to slurp water from his bowl. His slurping sounds competed with transistor radio sounds.

Pete grabbed a broken cookie from a box under his chair. He bit into the cookie and said, "It's supposed to be cold but sunny all weekend. I wonder why all this gloomy stuff is still hanging around like a blanket."

"So we don't have to roast in the sun?" I asked, grinned, and pulled up the collar on my red sweater. "Right now, we really do have it made in the shade. Brrr."

Pete glanced up and said, "I guess the sun *is* trying to make the scene by peeking out of those last few clouds. At least it stopped raining yesterday, and the Santa Ana winds aren't blowing away our baked goods . . . and our customers."

Buddy barked out several woofs like he understood Pete's words.

"The 'blanket of gloom' hasn't kept the customers away. We've made thirty dollars," I said.

"Yeah," said Pete. "And we've sold ten tickets for our pageant."

I picked up a pageant ticket from the pile and said, "You did a great job on these. I like the name . . . The Cool Christmas Pageant. I hope we get everything done for it. And I really hope we can give lots of money to the Community Chest."

"Yeah, me too," said Pete. "Now that your play's done, we can fill the parts next week and start rehearsals. Mary Jane is all geared up to direct everyone. She thinks she's the director, producer, manager, and one of the main actors in the pageant!"

"She is," I said as some of Dan's customers walked in our direction. "Are you going to tell her no? She'll go ape on us . . . get really angry. And she'd do all those jobs anyway. So why not give them to her? This is the giving season, and we need all the help we can get." I smiled up at our new customers and asked, "Can I help you?"

We happily sold more baked goods and pageant tickets. After the customers left, Buddy barked for attention and turned around. Then he wagged his white-tipped tail, rolled over on the asphalt parking lot, and played dead . . . for a few seconds. He popped back up and waited for his treat as we waited for more business.

"Buddy is such an actor," said Pete as we listened to my little doggy crunching treats in his mouth. "The good news is we could bring him with us today because he listens to commands. He's our greeter and treat eater."

"Buddy has a twin in the greeting and eating spotlight," I said as I pointed at Pete. "It's you!"

"Gee, thanks, Carol Ann," said Pete with a laugh as he crunched a cookie.

I smiled at Pete then down at our little beagle greeter. "With Mom's help, I baked Buddy special, decorated doggy biscuits. He's crunching one right now. I'll bake a bunch more for his birthday on Christmas day."

"I dig that idea," said Pete, "as long as you don't forget to bake special people treats for our Christmas day party in my backyard."

I left my chair and moved to the front of our table that looked like an outdoor bakery. Its white tablecloth cascaded to the ground. "Deck the Halls with Boughs of Holly" blasted from the radio. Red and green ribbon, attached to the table front, draped from each side of a big BAKE SALE sign. Red bows decorated the table corners.

Pete turned to the live Christmas tree on the table and adjusted a candy cane. "I like how you decorated this little tree with cookies and candy. The art you drew on our sign for your play looks really cool, too."

"Thanks, Pete," I said as a group of people headed our way for some of our goodies. After they left I said, "Do you think Dan's Diner is in the Annual Yule Decoration Contest for the business with the best light display? The contest is sponsored by the El Monte Kiwanis Club. My mom read about the contest in the paper."

"I don't know, but it should be," said Pete as he eyeballed the diner. "Dan sure put up a ton of decorations this year. They look unreal . . . really nice. I hope he enters."

"Dan should *win* the contest," I said. "He has hundreds of multi-colored lights around his windows and diner signs. The evergreen wreath on his front door looks nice against the black and white checkerboard entrance. Dan even stenciled his windows with cute Christmas designs."

Pete said, "Those decorated trees and outdoor lights look boss at night. Oops, I almost forgot this." Pete dug in his pocket and brought out an article from the newspaper. He read, "COMMUNITY CHEST NEEDS HELP." Then he glanced up and said, "They help Campfire Girls, all the scout troops, the children's hospital, a community center, Family Service, the Community Welfare Association, and Catholic Welfare."

"Pete," I asked in a worried tone, "can we really do a pageant? We're only kids."

"Don't worry, Carol Ann. Our folks and neighbors will help us," said Pete. "And we have Mary Jane to organize us. How can we lose?"

More customers arrived, so I couldn't answer him. Pete helped me box up the two dozen cupcakes they bought. Cute, little Buddy got much-needed pats on his head and tickles to his tummy while "Twelve Days of Christmas" played on the radio.

"Would you like to buy tickets to our pageant?" Pete asked our customers. "The money is going to the Community Chest." They handed us money and left with tickets, cupcakes, and smiles.

"I've heard people talking about freezing some of their baked goods for holiday parties," I said. "That's a good idea!"

"Mom's got a boatload of frozen baked goods in our freezer. But I bet lots of the stuff bought today isn't going to make it to the freezer," said Pete as he licked frosting off a cupcake.

VROOM, VROOM, VROOM. Hawk's Ride rolled into a parking space next to our table. Ernie's 1932, black Ford Hi-boy called Wild Panther rolled into one across the way. The teens and Mary Jane climbed from the cars and headed in our direction.

Mary Jane looked really cute in a pink, wool coat dress with white, fake fur trim and a matching, fake fur hat. She balanced a tray in her out-stretched arms as she approached our bake sale table. She looked back at the teens and tripped. Cookies flew everywhere like chocolate-studded "flying saucers."

Buddy barked with double woofs as Mary Jane landed next to him on a pile of wrapped packages sitting near the corner of our table. She sputtered then screamed when the chocolate-studded cookies used her back as a landing field.

Pete and I rushed around the table as Hawk stepped over and lifted his sister up. He brushed off the front of her dress and picked "flying saucers" out of her hat. We didn't dare laugh even though her skip, jump, and fall had looked like a funny acrobatic act.

Mary Jane sputtered again, looked down at her cookie-coated dress, and wailed, "Oh, look at my new dress! It's full of cookie crumbs. Carol Ann's dirty, little dog tripped me! Then that mangy mutt tried to lick my face! Yuk!"

Pete pointed down at the asphalt parking lot and said, "Sorry, Sis, but you took a tumble on that dirty, little crack down there when you weren't looking."

As the song, "Jingle Bells," jingled around the parking lot, Mary Jane pointed and said, "Well, that dog would have tripped me if he could have." She glared down at Buddy who slunk under the tablecloth to hide out with our extra baked goods and the rest of his decorated dog biscuits.

Hawk, Ernie, and Tim picked up broken cookies and tried not to laugh at Mary Jane's tantrum. Like a blessing from heaven, sun rays poured down on our bake sale.

Pete smiled and said sweetly, "Mary Jane, it looks like you brought the sunshine with your smiling face . . . oops, I mean your frowning face that's going to smile."

Mary Jane gave Pete a dirty look and said, "I'm getting the rest of our baked goods from Hawk's Ride, so keep that dirty dog out of my way."

Hawk said, "Those are some good sounds coming out of my radio. Like wow! I dig Christmas music."

"Thanks for letting us use it," said Pete as he looked towards Mary Jane. "It helps the atmosphere, especially when storm clouds are approaching!"

I looked up at the sunny sky with a frown then realized Pete was talking about Mary Jane who now approached carrying a big box. She set it down behind the table, rearranged the table-top, and sat down on one of our three folding chairs.

A car pulled up with two of our classmates inside. Angela Atwood and Neil Caruso got out and carried trays towards us. Then Adam's mom dropped him off. *That's nice of them to want to help after Pete and Stu told our class about our fundraising idea.*

Mary Jane said with a wave and a friendly smile, "Hi Angela, Neil, and Adam. Thanks for helping. Now, have a seat next to me, and we'll take care of the bake sale. Pete, you and Carol Ann can go to lunch. And be sure to take that mangy mutt with you."

I retrieved Buddy's leash and said to him, "Let's go have lunch."

Buddy followed us as we followed Hawk and his friends to the diner entrance. I hooked Buddy's leash to one of Dan's decorated outdoor Christmas trees. He hunkered down next to his food and water bowls. The shade under the tree protected him from the sun.

Inside the diner, yummy aromas greeted my nose. I stepped with Pete across the black and white checkerboard floor to a booth. We scooted around on the red vinyl benches. I picked up a menu from the round, chrome-edged table. Customers sat at booths or on red and chrome chairs at round tables scattered throughout the room.

The record, "Have Yourself a Merry Little Christmas," by Judy Garland, played on the jukebox in the back corner next to a tree with ornaments and sparkling multi-colored lights. Boughs of plastic holly and red bows decorated the wall behind the counter.

Dan waved to us from the kitchen window where he cooked his "fabulous food." That's what Uncle Charlie liked to say. Soon, a waitress in a red-striped uniform covered by a crisp, white apron took our lunch orders.

The teens teased and laughed at each other. Tim drummed his fingers on the table to the song, "I Want a Hippopotamus for Christmas." *Tim and his crutches remind me of Tiny Tim from the Charles Dickens's novel,* A Christmas Carol. *Can our fundraising money help Tim get more therapy so that someday his crippled legs can walk without crutches?*

The giant, green milkshake machine *whirred* as it spun ice

cream, milk, and flavorings into silky, smooth shakes. *Yum.* Edith and her dad entered the diner and took seats at the counter. Dan, the owner and a Marine, visited our table with a tray of food for us. A smiling waitress followed close behind him.

As they unloaded our lunch, Dan said, "It looks like you're having a successful bake sale outside. Tomorrow and next weekend should be equally busy. I'll help you out and buy pageant tickets for my whole work crew."

"Thanks, Dan," said Pete after swallowing a burger bite. "That's really cool."

"Merry Christmas," said Dan as he headed back to his kitchen.

We finished eating our food, gathered our jackets and sweaters, and slipped between the tables to the exit. "We Three Ships" played on the jukebox. *The teens are like three ships, and one of them is listing as he navigates with his crutches,* I thought.

Back outside, I untied Buddy, grabbed his empty bowls, and hurried back to the bake sale. Happy customers passed by us with holiday treats.

Pete sang along with the song on the radio, "It's Beginning to Look a Lot like Christmas." He waved at Edith as she approached us and said, "Hi, Edith, are you here to help?" She nodded yes.

Hawk said, "We gotta split, but we'll be back to pick you up at four p.m. Be successful."

■   ■   ■

After Hawk cut out of the parking lot and many customers later, Pete took the cash box over by one of the outdoor Christmas trees. He counted our treasure for the Community Chest. *He's grinning,* I thought. *We did well today. Yea!*

He brought the cash box back and slid it under the tablecloth as we packed up the leftovers for tomorrow's sale. Mary Jane,

Neil, Angela, Edith, and Adam bustled around boxing up goodies while I took Buddy for a short trot around the diner.

"Hurry, Buddy, so we can help pack up the bake sale and your stuff that's stashed under the table," I said as I raced my doggy back to help our helpers.

As Mary Jane took down our BAKE SALE sign she said to Pete, "I told you Mom's Eggnog Pies would sell." Pete made a yucky face. "She found that recipe in the *El Monte Herald* and made up a couple of them. They smelled like nutmeg."

"That's cool. But I don't eat eggnog, nutmeg stuff," said Pete.

Mary Jane narrowed her eyes at me and snarled, "Yes, and normally I wouldn't eat a disgusting dog biscuit disguised as a cookie. Yuk!"

Just in time, Hawk's Ride roared into the parking lot right at 4:00 p.m. We loaded up the trunk, said goodbye to our classmates, and climbed into the back seat. Pete clutched our cash box to his chest. I settled Buddy on the floor at our feet where he sniffed around. Hawk fired up the hot rod and rolled out of the Dan's Diner parking lot.

Pete leaned back on the seat and whispered, "I wonder where Hawk and his friends went today? It's the case of the disappearing teens."

I leaned back on the seat and thought about our bake sale and the case of the decorated dog biscuit that ended up in Mary Jane's mouth. Yikes! *Except for that, we did well today. But will our bake sale do as well tomorrow? Can we earn enough money to really help poor people? Are Hawk and his friends doing something bad?*

5

Decorating Day

"Yea! Today is decorating day!" I yelled to Pete as he slipped through the gate between our yards. He ran with Buddy under the clothesline and past the chicken car. The afternoon breeze brushed at my hair bringing chicken smells to my nose.

"Are you gonna decorate the chicken car?" asked Pete as he looked down at Buddy. "Carol Ann likes to decorate everything." Buddy woofed in agreement.

"I thought about putting an evergreen wreath on that old car's front grill to make it more festive and to make it smell better," I said as we sat down on two swings hanging from our swing set. Buddy sniffed around the chicken car with a snuffling noise.

Our feet seemed to brush against the blue sky as we swung up then back down again. Before we could brush the sky too many times, the little kids swarmed around us. They climbed onto the monkey bars and hung upside-down. Gail scampered up the steps of our slide and sat on top waiting to slide down.

She called to me, "Hey, Carol Ann, watch me slider down to the ground."

Pete called out, "We're watching, Gail. Have a fun time *sliddering.*"

Pete's little sister, Mandy, followed Gail and so did Little Charlie and Cathie. They looked like a sliding kid parade. *They will be cute in our pageant parade*, I thought.

"When's your dad taking us to the tree lot in downtown El Monte?" asked Pete.

"Any minute he'll be out and ready to leave," I answered. "I'm glad your mom is letting you and Mandy ride along with us to buy our Christmas tree."

"I'm glad, too," said Pete as he swung around on his swing making circles in the dirt. Pete frowned and said, "I've got bad news for you, Carol Ann."

I stopped circling, looked at Pete, and said, "What happened?"

Pete said, "Some money is missing from our bake sale gig yesterday. Remember when I counted the money then put the cash box back under the table? Well, there's twenty dollars missing from the box! Someone dipped in there while we cleaned up and our backs were turned. Do you have your notepad handy? Write down some clues."

"That's terrible," I said as I pulled my notepad and pencil from my pocket. I flipped the notepad open to a clean sheet. "I'm ready. Tell me what to write."

"Write down that twenty dollars of bake sale money is missing from our sale on December tenth," said Pete. "And list the names of everyone who helped: Mary Jane, Neil, Angela, Adam, Edith, and an unknown crook or crooks."

I concentrated on listing the names and said, "But Buddy would have barked if crooks came up and snooped around in our stuff."

"Some strangers did snoop around in our stuff while you walked Buddy around the diner. They offered to help us. Did they help themselves to our twenty dollars?"

"I hope that strangers are the crooks and not someone we know!" I said. "That's awful, Pete. We have to watch our money like . . . hawks."

Pete smiled at that as my dad dashed down the sidewalk and

waved for us to follow him. He looked tall, dark, and handsome in his black slacks and gray, collared, long-sleeved shirt. Dad loaded us into Mom's Hudson Jet for the ride downtown.

From the back seat, we watched the houses on our street flash by. Wreaths decorated their doors, and outdoor lights outlined their roofs. Dad cut out onto Peck Road on his way to El Monte's downtown, passing tall buildings on each side of the street. He pulled into the tree lot next to a grocery store.

As we climbed out of Mom's car, Pete said, "Like unreal, like wow! Look at that forest of Christmas trees they've got set up. And, hey, there's Hawk."

Pete greeted Hawk and his friends. A pungent, pine forest fragrance wafted to my nose. I took a deep breath savoring the smell as I followed Dad through the aisles of trees. *This smells like the forest at Santa's Village.*

The Christmas song, "Happy Holidays," by Bing Crosby, soared over our heads from loud speakers. Happy families roamed throughout the forest of cut trees displayed on the dirt parking lot.

Dad circled a seven-foot tree with a perfect shape and said, "I like this one. What do you think? Shall we get it?"

Like the church choir this morning, we sang out, "We like it! Yeah, let's get it!"

And we did. The nice salesman took Dad's money then helped Dad strap the tree to the top of Mom's car. We popped back into the car for our ride home. Pretty Christmas decorations adorned all the storefronts along the downtown street.

"Did your brother pick out a tree for your house?" I asked.

Pete said, "Hawk found a really boss tree that he loaded into the rumble seat of Ernie's '32. I hope it makes it home 'cause Ernie's souped-up car drives like a rocket."

"If Ernie cuts his rocket power, the tree should make it," I said with a smile.

Pete pointed at a line of people on the sidewalk, "It looks like Santa Claus is hanging out in front of the department store. I'm glad we're not waiting in that *long* line."

As Dad slowed down for traffic, I watched Santa's elves herding kids forward like cattle in a line. The Salvation Army lady rang her bell seeking money donations to help the poor. Stenciled windows, wreaths with red bows, and winter scenes decorated the store-fronts of each downtown business.

Gail said, "I want that fanciest dress in that window and a new dolly carraiger."

Kathleen said, "Say doll carriage." Gail tried to say it without success.

■　■　■

Back at home, we carried the Christmas tree into our house, getting sticky, pine-scented tree sap on our hands. Dad set the tree up in a metal stand while we opened boxes filled with decorations from past Christmases. Mom's record player played, "There's No Place like Home for the Holidays," from Perry Como's Christmas album.

Buddy barked from outside. Then he howled excitedly like a hound dog with a rabbit cornered in a hole. I left the excitement in our living room for the excitement on our front porch.

I opened the door, bent down, patted my doggy's head, and said, "Hi, Buddy, what are you so excited about? Do you want me to decorate your dog house?" Buddy wagged his tail and woofed at me.

Pete said, "You fracture me. I knew you would decorate his dog house."

Mom smiled at us and said, "That's our girl. Carol Ann likes to decorate everything at Christmastime. I let her, so I have more time to take care of the kids."

"And Mrs. H, that also gives you time to bake cookies for your favorite neighbor," said Pete pointing to himself with a grinning face.

Mom smiled back at him as she entered her kitchen and said, "Now that you mention it, I have cookies and milk for everyone . . . after the tree is decorated."

Pete said, "Thanks, Mrs. H." He turned to me and said, "Your mom is so hip." Buddy barked from his place on the front doormat.

"Buddy agrees with you," I said as I dug into a box full of tangled lights.

Pete helped me untangle the colorful light strands so Dad could string them on the tree. Dad finished the lights, plugged them in, and stood back to look at the magic. The Christmas tree sparkled with multi-colored orbs and bubble lights. Each bubble light sent bubbling liquid up a see-through tube from a glass bulb attached to a tree branch.

"Now, let's carefully put the glass ornaments on each branch," I said to the little kids. I reached into a large cardboard box and brought out smaller boxes. Delicate glass ornaments nestled between cardboard dividers like colorful eggs in egg cartons.

"The Christmas Song," by Nat King Cole, played on the stereo. Dad sang along with his deep, rich voice that sounded like Mr. Cole. Dad sang, "Chestnuts roasting on an open fire, Jack Frost nipping at your nose. Tiny tots with their eyes all aglow . . ."

When the song ended, I said, "Wow, Dad, you sing like Nat King Cole. Could you please sing that song for our pageant?"

Dad smiled and said, "Sure, I'd love to sing for your pageant. Count me in."

I helped the kids hang pretty ornaments on the tree. My favorite ones, the red-colored glass with white glitter, looked like frosty snow had permanently dripped on them. Other ornaments had indents that sparkled like kaleidoscopes.

After all the ornaments, candy canes, and homemade school art found places on the tree, I opened boxes of silver tinsel. The little kids watched as Pete and I tediously strung skinny, silver tinsel strands onto each tip of each tree branch.

"It's beautiful," I said to Pete. "Thanks for helping to make our tree sparkle."

"Anytime, Carol Ann," said Pete. "I especially like to help when I'm rewarded with your mom's freshly-baked, hot-out-of-the-oven chocolate chip cookies."

"Before we eat cookies, help me get out our stockings," I said. "Then the kids can hang them up on our cardboard fireplace that Dad brought home from his work."

"Okay," said Pete. "You're the only family I know with a cardboard fireplace."

"Then our family is unique," I said as I lifted our four felt-appliquéd Christmas stockings out of a box. "Here they are, Kids. Hang them up on our *special* fireplace while I get out the candles, holders, and plastic holly to decorate the mantel."

"I sure hope you don't light those candles while they're sitting on that cardboard mantel," said Pete as I arranged the green plastic holly with its red berries. Then I placed pretty Christmas cards in and out of the greenery.

"We don't light these candles," I said while nestling them in the holly on each side of the mantel. Then I added big, red bows at each corner.

Reaching into one of the storage boxes, I retrieved twelve three-inch, ceramic pixies that Mom made years ago in a ceramics class. When I arranged them in white batting along the windowsill of our picture window, they seemed to frolic in the fake snow.

Pete handed me a plastic holly wreath and said, "Where does this go?"

Buddy looked up at me as I hung the wreath on our front door. "Hey, Buddy, I've got one like this for your dog house," I said. "And I've got good treats for you, too. Meet me out back on the patio."

My hound dog scampered off the front porch and disappeared.

After meeting Buddy on the back porch and hanging the wreath on his beat-up dog house, we all enjoyed a cookie snack. Then I escorted Pete and Mandy home across our grass and past the slide, swings, and monkey bars.

Mary Jane waited at the gate and said, "It's about time you two headed for home. I called for you an hour ago. Don't you want to help decorate the tree that Hawk got us?"

"Sure, Sis," said Pete. "We're ready and able to decorate the tree."

"Oh, and by the way, Carol Ann, when do I get to read your play?" asked Mary Jane. "I need to look it over and see if it will work for the pageant."

"Wait a minute, Sis. It's working for the pageant because it's *cool* and Carol Ann wrote it," said Pete. "So when you read it, you'll love it. Keep that in mind."

Mary Jane held up her hands and said, "Okay, fine! I'll read the play and figure out who fits the parts. Let's go home, Mandy," said Mary Jane as she took Mandy's hand and stomped away.

"Thanks for sticking up for me, Pete," I said. "I hope your sister likes the play."

"She tried to put you down again, so I stopped her," said Pete. "Mom's been working with Mary Jane about her bullying. Maybe it's working. I gotta split and help string lights on our Christmas tree. See ya later, alligator."

"After while, crocodile, and happy decorating day," I said as Pete bolted through the gate. "Let's go back home, Buddy, to see what else needs decorating."

Buddy trotted after me on his short doggy legs while he stopped occasionally to sniff the grass tufts along the edge of the sidewalk.

I asked Buddy, "Do you think Mary Jane will like my wild idea for a play about animals and the baby Jesus? I hope so, or we're shot down . . . sunk."

6

Christmas Tree Lane

"Christmas Can't Be Far Away," sang a man from Uncle Charlie's radio on the dashboard of his big, black Plymouth sedan. My uncle cruised along Huntington Drive in San Moreno on our way to Lacy Park. *After that, he's taking us to see the Christmas lights on Christmas Tree Lane in the city of Altadena. Yea!*

Uncle Charlie had loaded us into his car right after school. Then he had cut out of our neighborhood for a fun adventure on a school night. He had turned onto Peck Road in El Monte, then to Santa Anita Avenue, and had turned left onto Huntington Drive.

Pete leaned over to me and said, "Huntington Drive is so wide it's like a highway. Hey, look at the cool decorations on all the businesses."

Buddy looked up at me, leaned his beagle head sideways, and listened to Pete talk. I patted Buddy's head and said, "Uncle Charlie always takes us this way to Lacy Park, then to his folks' house. They're traveling, so we won't visit them today."

Buddy sniffed at the cool afternoon breeze wafting through the partially open window on my uncle's tank. Tall trees lined the wide street. In the distant western sky, bumpy cotton-ball-clouds glowed pink, purple, and silver.

I pointed at the sky and asked Pete, "Is that the silver lining in the clouds?"

"It sure does look like silver," said Pete. "Speaking of silver linings, things are moving right along for our Cool Christmas Pageant. Sometimes it's good to have a take-charge sister. Yeah, she's charging ahead like a hopped-up hot rod at the drag strip."

I said, "The meeting on Monday with the neighborhood kids and our friends went really well. I think this pageant is going to be successful, but I can't help worrying."

"Dig out your notepad, and look up one of those Bible verses you wrote down," said Pete. "What about the one that says, 'Be strong and of good courage?'"

"That's Joshua 1:9, and I like it," I said as I pulled my notepad from my pocket and flipped a few pages. "I wrote down another verse that should also help me. It's from Nehemiah 8:10 and at the end of the verse it says, '. . . the joy of the LORD is my strength.'"

"So, Carol Ann," said Pete. "Have a little strength, joy, and faith that we can do a pageant."

"I'll work on it," I said. "Nehemiah in the Bible had a project to rebuild the stone walls around Jerusalem to help the people of that city. And we have a project to build a stage and a production to help people in our city. Nehemiah and his crew knew that the joy of the LORD was their strength."

"Cool rhyme, Carol Ann," said Pete.

Another Christmas tune circled the car as Ella Fitzgerald sang, "Santa Claus Got Stuck in My Chimney." The little kids laughed at the words to the silly song. Buddy woofed at the silly kids.

Pete said, "Santa can't get stuck in your fireplace 'cause it doesn't have a chimney."

I looked at Pete with bulging eyes and said, "Santa Claus walks through the front door at our house, so we don't need a chimney."

"That's right, Carol Ann," said Uncle Charlie from the front seat. "Even though "Dear Old Gal" and I have a fireplace with a chimney, Santa still uses our front door sometimes." He grinned at me in his rearview mirror as the kids smiled with satisfaction.

Gail said, "I'm glad Santy Claude can't get stuck in a chimney like in the song."

The tank slowed down and made a right turn at Virginia Road. Uncle Charlie motored up the street past *very* nice homes, circled Lacy Park, then parked along the curb.

"We've got an hour here before dark," he warned us.

Once outside the car, Pete and I took off after Buddy on his leash. We left Buddy tied to a tree on the hilltop while we rolled down the grassy hill like Jack and Jill taking a tumble. Buddy howled at us as we scrambled up to him. Then he danced like a wiggly worm, rolled over, and popped up again.

Behind the trees, the sunset glowed in vivid colors. Dark shadows filled the park as we raced through the trees and around the bushes. Uncle Charlie yelled, "hide and seek," hid his face against a tree, and started counting as we hurried to hiding spots. He finished counting and yelled, "READY OR NOT, I'LL FIND YOU!"

Clad in his tan pants, tan shirt, and pith helmet, Uncle Charlie searched for us like a guide on a jungle safari. Late afternoon shadows disguised us, but my uncle still spotted Little Charlie. He crept up to his hiding place and shouted, "TAG, YOU'RE IT!"

My cousin squealed like a surprised piglet as he plunged from his hiding place to become the hunter rather than the hunted. We played Hide and Seek until the last rays of sunshine disappeared from the western sky. Evening shadows merged together and bathed the park in inky darkness.

"Last one to the car is a rotten egg," said Uncle Charlie as he dashed for his auto.

We panted like puppies as we climbed into the Plymouth and relaxed on the scratchy, gray upholstery. Pete tucked his plaid shirt into his jeans as I adjusted my sweater. I patted my notepad and pencil in my jeans pocket. Then I patted Buddy as the tank agitated the gravel next to the curb and split for Christmas Tree Lane.

"That was a blast," said Pete. "What a cool place. Mom said this park is above Pasadena and Hollywood. It's not far from The Santa Claus Lane Parade that we go see every year on Thanksgiving weekend. The parade is a kick to watch."

Just then, "Here Comes Santa Claus," by Gene Autry, filled the car with sound. The little kids sang along as Uncle Charlie turned right and left onto several streets. We "ooohhed" and "ahhhhed" as he drove past homes decorated in sparkling lights.

We passed a huge, ornate gate and fence on Oxford Road. Uncle Charlie slowed down and said, "That's Huntington Library and Gardens. It was the home of Mr. Henry E. Huntington who died in 1927. He willed the buildings, art, manuscripts, and one hundred and fifty acres of gorgeous gardens to the city of San Marino. The buildings and gardens are open to the public."

"That was so nice of him," I said. "Can we visit there sometime?"

"Sure," said my uncle as he turned his car to climb the hill. "The famous paintings, Blue Boy and Pinkie, are there as well as a Gutenberg Bible and letters written by Presidents Washington, Jefferson, Lincoln, and the statesman, Benjamin Franklin."

Gail spoke up and said, "I wanna see the blue boy and his girlfriend, Pinkie."

We tried not to laugh at my sister as Uncle Charlie drove up, up, up, to the city of Altadena located north of Los Angeles in the foothills of the San Gabriel Mountains. *If it wasn't dark outside, I could see the snow sitting on the mountain tops.* We stopped at a cute café in Altadena for dinner. We ate, left the café, and paraded like stuffed snowmen out to the tank.

As Uncle Charlie drove up the hill, an orange, flame-painted hot rod passed us going downhill. Pete said, "Like wow! Look at that chrome-plated, cherry machine. What a classy chassis!"

Uncle Charlie nodded with a smile and said, "I've got a surprise for you, Kiddos."

Cousin Cathie said, "What's our surprise, Daddy? Is it a dolly?"

Uncle Charlie said, "Before we go to Christmas Tree Lane, we're stopping at the Balian Mansion that's just a block off of this street."

Little Charlie groaned and said, "Aw gee, Dad, have we gotta stop?"

"You'll want to stop when you see this place," said my uncle as he rounded the corner. We gasped at the light display in front of us.

Millions of white lights draped the enormous Balian Mansion and its grounds. The lights attached to the house formed the shapes of giant, triangular Christmas trees. A car parked in front pulled away from the curb, so my uncle pulled into that spot. We sat in wild-eyed wonder as we eyeballed a sparkling spectacle of lights before us.

Pete spoke up first, "Like crazy, like wow! It's unreal! It's boss! I'm glad we got to make the scene. Can we get out and walk around, Dr. Charles?"

"We sure can," said my uncle as he opened his driver's side door. "You Kiddos need to hold hands as we move around this place so you don't get lost."

"Let's go, Buddy," I said as we left the car. Buddy howled in awe and wonder.

Pete said, "If I was a dog, I'd howl, too. Those are the coolest illuminations on a house that I've ever seen. This is Fat City . . . another cool place like Santa's Village."

A nativity scene had been set up on the grass of the mansion's left side. It drew us to its realistic portrayal of Jesus's birth. "Silent Night, Holy Night" played on loud speakers as we quietly approached. Spotlights illuminated the realistic cut-outs of Joseph, Mary, Wise Men with their camels, stable animals, and baby Jesus in the manger.

"This is so beautiful," I whispered. "Could my play look like this?"

"It can," said Pete. "It will tell the story of King Jesus born in a humble stable."

I whispered, "He's Immanuel, God with us. John 3:16 says, 'For God so loved the world, that he gave his only begotten Son, that whosoever believeth in him should not perish, but have everlasting life.'" Buddy sniffed at the animal cut-outs in the manger.

After enjoying the lighted displays on the lawn, we climbed back into the car. As my uncle pulled away from the Balian Mansion, the song, "What Child is This?" floated inside.

"That was fabulous," said Uncle Charlie. "Did you like my surprise?"

"Yes," we chorused as one voice then sang, "What Child is This?"

Back on North Allen Road, Uncle Charlie floored it to get his tank up the rest of the hill. We passed more lovely, lighted houses but nothing like the Balian Mansion with its ultimate Christmas display.

"We're almost to the other surprise," said my uncle as he turned left at East Altadena Drive. The little kids wiggled around in anticipation while the car cruised along. "Are you ready for the second surprise?"

His daughter Cathie said, "I'm ready, Daddy. Can we see the lane?"

"In a minute," replied her dad. "Christmas Tree Lane is a mile-long street lined on both sides by more than a hundred lighted Deodar Cedar trees that have grown over one hundred and twenty feet tall. Every year, since 1920, the trees have been strung with multi-colored lights. This street is one of the oldest, lighted Christmas holiday displays in California."

Pete said, "These light displays remind me of God's light display . . . the stars."

Anticipation filled the car as it slowed to a stop and paused to turn left onto Santa Rosa Avenue. Uncle Charlie turned the wheel. Surprise! Christmas Tree Lane glowed gloriously down the hill in front of us. The Deodar trees soared into the night sky with lights cascading from top to bottom forming multi-colored triangles.

Pete said, "Wow! I dig these trees! Look how high those lights soar into the sky. I'm gonna tell Hawk to cruise Christmas Tree Lane."

The little kids squirmed to the windows to see the decorated Deodar trees as we rolled slowly down Santa Rosa Avenue. Icy wind *wooshing* down from the snow-covered San Gabriel's stirred and rocked the tall trees. Buddy howled at the moving giants.

As we passed the last trees on Christmas Tree Lane, I waved goodbye. "O Holy Night" softly played on the radio as we sat back for the ride home. In mere minutes, the little kids nodded off, including Buddy who had curled up next to my feet. *It's only 7:30 p.m., and we'll be home in a little while,* I thought. *I'm glad I don't have any homework.*

Uncle Charlie drove down from the hills and turned onto Foothill Boulevard, also known as Route 66. Pete and I whispered back and forth, so we didn't wake up the little sleepers.

"Thanks for inviting me along, Carol Ann," said Pete. "I'm gonna tell Mom about our adventure tonight. She'll want to see that Balian Mansion."

"I loved all the lights on the house and the nativity scene," I said. "With everyone's help, I hope we can recreate a beautiful manger scene for our pageant."

"No sweat, Carol Ann," said Pete. "Mary Jane is organizing everything. Our moms are sewing curtains and costumes. Adam's dad is building the stage this weekend, and Tim is painting all our backdrops. We've got it made."

"I'm praying that's true and nothing gets messed up," I said. "Is our money from both bake sales in a safe place? We can't afford more missing money."

"The bake sale money is safe, but I'm missing the dollar I left in my school desk for a trap," said Pete. "The problem is, I didn't trap anyone."

"I wish we didn't have to worry about traps, crooks, and gathering clues," I said.

Pete said, "The newspaper says that there are crooks everywhere."

Uncle Charlie heard our whispers and said, "That's for sure. In yesterday's paper, there were reports of two burglaries. But there were dozens of articles about good things. Students from three local high schools are aiding the needy like you're doing. And the police are having a dance at Legion Stadium to aid the local police and fire charities."

"I'm glad our community helps one another," I said. "That's the royal law in the Bible. We're supposed to love our neighbors."

Pete said, "It's really neighborly for the El Monte community to put on the annual Children's Christmas Party gig at American Legion Stadium on December eighteenth. There's gonna be decorated Christmas trees and candy bags for all the kids. Of course their trees won't be as good as the ones on Christmas Tree Lane."

"Those trees are the best," I said as my uncle pulled into our driveway. "Thanks, Uncle Charlie, for the fun time."

Pete said, "Thanks, Dr. Charles, for inviting me. I'll walk Carol Ann home."

As we approached my lighted porch, Pete stopped, stepped onto the grass, and looked up at the night sky. I moved off of the sidewalk, stood where I couldn't see the porch light, and looked up. Buddy sat down, looked at us, then he looked up, too.

"Pete, what are you looking at?" I asked.

"I'm looking at the stars," answered Pete. "The lights on the Balian Mansion and Christmas Tree Lane made me think about the lights in the night sky. Since it's a new moon tonight, which we can't see, the stars look extra bright." Buddy dropped down on the grass and flipped on his back to view the sparkly stars.

"I wish I knew their names," I said. "I do know Bible verses about the stars in Psalm 19. They say, 'The heavens declare the glory of God; and the firmament sheweth his handywork. Day unto day uttereth speech, and night unto night sheweth knowledge.'"

"My gramps knows those same verses," said Pete. "He's an amateur astronomer, and he knows the stars names, their decans, and the constellations they belong to. Do you see those three stars up there? That's Orion's Belt. He's a mighty warrior in the sky."

"Gosh, Pete, I didn't know you knew about the stars," I said. "I hope you'll share all you know about them with me someday."

"Sure, Carol Ann," said Pete. "My gramps told me that many of the star names are from the Bible. Someday, let's have Gramps tell us about God's story in the stars."

"That would be cool," I said as I got back on the sidewalk. "See ya."

"After while, Carol Ann and Buddy," said Pete as he cut out.

"This was a fun evening, Buddy," I said to my special, little buddy as I chased him to my front porch. "Be a good doggy and go get in your dog house. Goodnight." Buddy wagged his tail then disappeared around the corner into the darkness.

As I pulled open the front door, I thought, *I hope we have fun tomorrow after school while we work on our pageant.* As the door slammed behind me, I had one last thought. *Can we keep our money safe from crooks?*

7

A Cherrylee Christmas

"Hi-ho, Silver! Away!" yelled Pete as he galloped down his driveway and met me on our street. "I watched the *Lone Ranger* last night on TV."

"So did we," I said as I hitched my school bag higher up on my shoulder. I cradled a box of Mom's Christmas cookies in the crook of my arm. "It was a really cool episode."

Pete looked behind me and waved to Buddy who sat on the edge of the street. "See ya after school," said Pete. Buddy answered with a bark.

I smiled at my little hound dog and said in a serious but nice voice, "Go back home, Buddy, and get a treat from Mom." Buddy barked, scampered across the grass in front of Aunt Ruthie's house, and disappeared up the driveway.

Stu and the Bailey brothers joined us on La Madera Avenue as we walked to school. We all carried boxes or bags of goodies for our special class Christmas party. Early morning clouds filled the sky, and a breeze blew my hair around my head.

"I'm sure glad my Christmas coat is keeping me warm this morning," I said. "Every time I wear it, I'm grateful that Granny knit it for me."

Pete glanced at me and said, "You were embarrassed to wear it to Santa's Village. You said it was the wrong color and it was too bright."

"I know," I said. "I'm grateful now, and I love my warm coat."

"That was a wild day at Santa's Village," said Pete. "We threw snowballs and rode wild rides all day."

Stu said, "My folks are going to take us there sometime this month."

Bob Bailey looked over at his brother and said, "Our parents took us last year during a snowstorm that was *really* wild."

Pete held up his hands. "Count the other wild things going on during this wild winter: the wild rainy weather on the first of December and more bad weather since then, the wild-looking gray clouds overhead today, our wild pageant idea, and Mary Jane, the Wild Woman, who blows hot air through our house like wild Santa Ana winds!"

"Don't forget the wild kids at our wild rehearsals," I giggled.

Our group turned the corner onto The Wye and Pete said, "Yeah, and what about the wild crooks who are stealing our money from school and the bake sales."

Stu said, "That stuff does sound wild. I hope this winter settles down."

"If it doesn't settle down, what will the rest of December be like?" I asked.

As we approached the school, Pete said, "It will be bad if we don't catch the crooks."

Once in our classroom, we unloaded our stuff. Festive decorations adorned our classroom for our Christmas party. I glanced at my nativity art displayed on the bulletin board. *Last night, at Open House, Mom said my artwork looked lovely.*

Becky sat down at her desk next to mine and whispered, "At Open House last night, your dad looked *so* handsome. He could be a movie star."

"Thanks, Becky," I said with a smile. "He works with a lot of movie stars through his job as a salesman at Brunswick Corporation. He's just Dad to me." *Becky's compliment is nice. Are compliments a way to give to others? I'll write that down.*

Mrs. Rose passed out our corrected homework assignments. Her high heels clicked down my row as she gave out words of encouragement while placing papers on one desk after another.

She stopped at my desk, smiled, handed me some papers, and said, "Good job, Carol Ann. I can't wait to see your play in your pageant.."

Pete gave me a-thumbs-up and mouthed the word, "Cool."

Mrs. Rose strode back to the front of the classroom and said, "Students, I'm very proud of you. Every story and play was a delight to read. Keep up the good work." She sat down and said, "Who has a current event to share with the class?"

Eileen raised her hand and said, "I read an article in the paper this morning that said, 'Santa Claus will attend the annual Community Christmas Party on December eighteenth.'"

Another hand went up. Susan said, "Next week, on Tuesday, December twentieth, at 10:30 a.m., there will be a Special Holiday Story Hour at the library."

I raised my hand and waited for the nod from Mrs. Rose. Then I said, "The Ford Foundation gave a thirty-one thousand dollar grant to Sister Kenny Memorial Hospital to help polio victims. The paper said the grant was part of a half-a-million dollar giveaway." *Can that money help Tim?*

Angela raised her hand and said, "The newspaper had an article about decking your home with holly, tinsel, and lights for a warm, Yuletide look. We did that."

"Thank you, Angela, for sharing," said Mrs. Rose. "I read the paper this morning, too, and cut out the recipe for Festive Mincemeat Mold. I'm hoping my husband will like it. Now, let's work on math and history. Then after lunch we'll have our party."

Several hours later, we pushed our desks around in a circle

leaving plenty of room at the front of the classroom for our short performances. There was also plenty of room in the back for the refreshment table.

As Pete and I went to get our treats for the table, he whispered behind his hand, "I'm sure glad Mrs. Rose is making that Mincemeat Mold for her husband and not for her students. Yuk. That thing sounds like bad news."

We arranged our goodies on the festively decorated table next to cute cupcakes, cookies, and a punch-filled bowl. My decorated sugar cookies sat next to Pete's chocolate brownies. Angela contributed a decorated cake while Stu's baked goods looked like baked bads . . . severely smashed bar cookies. Adam set down cream cheese bars.

Mrs. Rose approached the table and said, "I have a surprise for you, Students."

She opened up a cake carrier and proudly displayed her . . . Festive Mincemeat Mold. *Yikes.* She carefully put it down in the middle of the table where it was surrounded by fake holly and red ribbons. I glanced at Pete as he eyeballed the brown, molded thing. His eyes looked as round as two frosted cupcakes with sprinkles!

"Like crazy," said Pete. "Your Mincemeat Mold looks like . . . a lot of work."

Whewww, was Pete going to say that the Mold looks like Buddy's smelly piles we clean up? I said, "Thank you, Mrs. Rose, for thinking of us."

She clapped her hands and said, "Please sit down at your desks, Students, so we can start our performances."

Different groups of students stood in front of the classroom and took turns singing or playing musical instruments. We heard many Christmas carols: "The First Noel," "It Came upon a Midnight Clear," "God Rest Ye Merry Gentlemen," "Jingle Bells," "Joy to the World," "What Child is This?," and "Drummer Boy" pounded out on a drum.

Edith got up and arranged a wooden manger in front of the class. She sat down as Angela and Neil took her place. Their costumes made them look like Mary and Joseph. They sang "Silent Night" while bending over the manger filled with straw. Angela's fancy, sparkly shoes showed under "Mary's" blue tunic. *Angela loves those shoes.*

Weeks ago, Mrs. Rose had asked our class to plan a class Christmas party and assign different groups to different jobs. Some kids had volunteered to sing and entertain the class while others, like Pete and his friends, had volunteered to do clean-up. *Lucky me, today I'm in charge of the dessert table.*

After the short performances, our class played games, exchanged gifts, and ate refreshments. Susan liked the embroidered hanky she got from me. I opened a gift from Edith wrapped in crumpled paper with a sad bow. As the paper fell away, I saw a used Raggedy Ann doll. *Poor Edith. I'm glad I got her gift and that Angela didn't!* I looked for Edith and smiled. She smiled back with grateful eyes.

The shrill sound of the school bell ended our school day. Mrs. Rose said, "Thank you, everyone, for a wonderful class party. Have a very Merry Christmas. I will see you back here on Tuesday, January third, 1956. Class dismissed."

We cut out of the classroom like rockets launched to the moon and rushed down The Wye to our homes. *It's rehearsal day at Pete's place . . . or pad . . . as he likes to call it.*

I resettled my school bag on my shoulder and pictured the goodies inside: wax paper-wrapped brownies, ribbon candy, my A+ play, and a used doll. I said to Pete, "Neil liked the flashlight he got from you. I'm glad I got Edith's gift of a well-worn doll. I feel sorry for her. The dress she wore swallowed her up. I hope her family gets help for Christmas."

"Neil thanked me," said Pete. "I feel bad for Edith, too, but I still think she took my pencils and lunch money out of my desk. She's a crook in my book."

"Just because she's poor doesn't make her a crook," I said. "She seems nice."

"Nice or not, she's on the list of the people who were the last ones in the classroom today," said Pete. "My teacher's gift was missing from my school bag, too. Someone took it!"

"Yikes," I said in surprise. "Are you sure you had it with you?"

"Mom tucked it into my school bag when I was leaving," said Pete with a frown.

I reached into my pocket and pulled out my red notepad and pencil. "Do you want me to write clues down?" I asked. "I'm ready."

"Yeah, write more clues down," said Pete as he looked at my notepad. "Well, the last people in our classroom before lunch are possible crooks. Write down Edith, Angela, Mrs. Rose, Neil and . . . Adam. They're all suspects."

Startled, I looked at Pete and said, "You don't think that Adam took your pencils, your lunch money, the bake sale money, and your present for Mrs. Rose, do you? I don't believe it. And Angela's family has money. She doesn't need to steal."

"I don't think Adam or Mrs. Rose took my stuff," admitted Pete. "And Angela is rich, so she doesn't need to steal. But they're our suspects, so let's watch them like two hawks sitting on a tree branch. We need to spot this party pooper crook . . . or crooks."

I smiled at that and said, "Okay. And let's keep writing down clues in case they point in a different direction. Maybe the clues will point to a stranger, like the janitor."

"It's a mystery we need to solve before anything else is missing," said Pete.

"Did you ever figure out the mystery of why Hawk and his friends are missing all the time like that day of the bake sale?" I asked. "It's the mystery of The Disappearing Hawk . . . and Friends."

"He won't tell me anything, but he still disappears every day with Tim and Ernie," said Pete. "I asked Hawk if they go out to the polio hospital to volunteer. They did that last week for a high school project. He leaves without telling me anything."

"As long as they're not getting into trouble, they can have their mystery," I said. "I read that article in the paper about El Monte High School students helping polio kids at Sister Kenny Hospital. That's cool. Why didn't you share that article in class?"

"I didn't share it 'cause I don't like to read out loud," shared Pete. "I need to remember that Bible verse about joy and strength."

"That's the verse we need as we work on the pageant," I said. Nehemiah 8:10 says, ' . . . the joy of the LORD is our strength.'"

Pete said, "We need to *be joyful* while working at another bake sale this weekend."

"And to watch our bake sale ticket money," I said as we approached our homes. "Did the tent get set up in your backyard today?"

"It'd better be set up for our rehearsal today, or Mary Jane will *go ape* and turn into a full-blown hurricane with gale-force winds," laughed Pete.

"I don't want to witness a Hurricane Mary Jane." I giggled at my rhyme.

As we entered Pete's driveway, the top of a tall, white tent towered over Pete's backyard. "Coolsville," said Pete. "That tent looks hip."

VROOM. VROOM. VROOM. Hawk's Ride cruised behind us onto the driveway and stopped. The crazy song, "Dig That Crazy Santa Claus," played on Hawk's car radio. The engine stopped rumbling, so the teens and Mary Jane climbed from the car. Tim limped toward us on his crutches. *Will the teens mysteriously split again?*

Inside the tent, Mary Jane produced a clipboard with a checklist as she paraded back and forth where the stage would be built. A pile of lumber for the stage rested in a heap to one side of a tall, canvas wall. Painted plywood leaned against another section of "wall." Mary Jane motioned us over to the grass in the tent's middle. We sat down and waited for instructions. *She's a serious director*, I thought as I patted Buddy.

Tim eased himself down on a folding chair and leaned his crutches against its back. Hawk and Ernie reclined on the grass after setting up a record player and plugging it into an extension cord. Mary Jane paced back and forth across her "stage."

"Listen up, Kids," said Pete's older sister. "We're here to rehearse for our Cool Christmas Pageant that takes place in this tent on December twenty-third. That's next week! We don't have much time to practice, so we have to be serious about rehearsals."

While Mary Jane organized the kids into groups, Pete whispered, "Sis is like a drill sergeant. She's got some jets for organizing people."

I looked at Pete and said, "What does 'jets' mean?"

Pete said very quietly. "Hawk told me that jets means *to have brains*."

"I get it," I said. "Mary Jane has the brains to get the job done."

As controlled chaos took over the tent, Mary Jane consulted her clip board, and soon the singing groups, musicians, and actors took their places and rehearsed. It sounded like a Cherrylee Christmas as our classmates sang the same songs from our class party.

Clever Mary Jane is taking good advantage of what these singers already know.

Neil and Angela sang a duet again as Mary and Joseph with the manger scene that Tim had painted. Edith played a Christmas tune on her beat-up guitar. The Bailey brothers rehearsed a funny new song called, "I'm Getting Nuttin' for Christmas."

We watched Hawk, Ernie, and Tim practice the spoof they dreamed up based on *A Christmas Carol*. I glanced at Pete and asked, "Are the teens disappearing to work on their version of Charles Dicken's book that we read in class last week?"

Before Pete could answer, Mary Jane waved at us and said, "I don't need you two right now, but I will shortly. Can you go find Adam for his singing part?"

"Sure thing, Sis," said Pete as we got up to go find Adam. "That's another mystery. Neil told me that Adam's a thief because he took money from *his* school desk."

Buddy ran ahead of us as we went through the gate and down the sidewalk to the backyard. We spotted the top of Adam's head bobbing along behind the bush-covered fence as he crossed Mr. Chester's backyard. "Do you believe Neil? I don't."

Pete shrugged and said, "Hey, Adam! Mary Jane sent us to find you."

"Hi," called Adam from behind the fence. "Help me with these curtains."

Adam struggled with a pile of dark fabric weighing down his arms as he pressed up to the fence corner. Pete opened up the secret, fake gate in our chain link fence that we shared with Mr. Chester. Adam ducked through the opening, and I grabbed curtains from the stack he held.

"Thanks for helping me," said Adam over the top of the fabric.

"No sweat," said Pete as he grabbed more of the pile. "Parade of the Wooden Soldiers" wafted over the fence from Mary Jane's record player.

Yikes. Pete thinks Adam took Neil's money. I don't believe it!

The way we stepped right now mimicked those wooden soldiers. We marched across my yard with our arms stretched out in front of us carrying stage curtains sewn by Adam's mom. *All we need are helmets and uniforms.*

At our gate, I heard Becky, Susan, and Eileen practicing the same song from our party at school. "We Three Kings of Orient

Are" made me smile and say a short prayer. *Thanks, God, for a Cherrylee Christmas times two. Please, God, help us to earn enough money from our pageant so we can help poor people. Please, please, God . . . keep Mary Jane happy.*

And please, please, please, God, help us to find the Christmas crooks. Is Adam our crook?

8

Two Christmas Parties

The song, "C-H-R-I-S-T-M-A-S," blared over the fence from Pete's yard. My friend opened the gate and strolled through it. Then Pete sat down on one of the swings dangling from our swing set. I admired his black slacks, white shirt, and tie. I smoothed down my red velvet party dress and touched matching bows in my hair that held back my brown waves.

"What's buzzin, cuzzin?" Pete asked me as Buddy scurried over and waited for a pat on the head. "Are you ready for the two parties today? Do you like my threads?"

"You look nice," I said as Pete patted Buddy then tickled the little hound's chin. "I'm ready for the Christmas parties, but the rest of the family is still *getting* ready."

"Yeah, my sisters were bugging me, so I cut out," said Pete. "They can't decide what to wear to the Community Christmas Party at the American Legion Stadium today. I told Mary Jane just to wear something *pink*. She tattled to Mom that I was making fun of her."

"Girls need more time and patience," I said. "That's something you could *give* them since we're in the *giving* season, and we're looking for unique ways to give."

"Aw, gee, Carol Ann," said Pete after swinging in a big circle. "Why'd ya have to remind me about giving? That it's not just about giving money and time."

"I'm reminding myself as well," I said. "Our pastor reminded us that God loves a cheerful giver, so I wrote the verse down in my notepad."

Pete said, "Are you ready for party number one at Legion Stadium?"

Buddy sat up and whined. I looked down and said, "Pete's not talking to you, Buddy. You have to guard our yard from rabbits, rodents, and other varmints."

Buddy howled with a serious sound to let us know he could scare off all intruders. He crouched down with his tail wagging behind him like a stick in the wind. Pete picked up a real stick and threw it. Buddy raced across the lawn like a hound in pursuit of a fox.

"El Monte's American Legion Stadium is a really cool place," said Pete. "My dad goes there for boxing matches and to watch Roller Derby."

"My dad does, too," I said. "My Aunt Jean, who lives in Long Beach, loves Roller Derby and the Thunderbirds' team."

"Legion Stadium has dances, too," said Pete. "Bands play rock 'n' roll music for the dancers. Hawk and his friends have been to a few. Hawk said that *anyone* is welcome to the dances at the Legion 'cause it's in the county of Los Angeles and not in the city. It doesn't matter what color your skin is as long as you pay to have a *blast*."

"That's cool," I said. "I wish I was old enough to go to dances."

"Not me," said Pete. "I'm still recovering from the square dancing I was forced to do at Knott's Berry Farm. I'm a *goof* at dancing." Buddy danced over to us with a stick in his mouth and waited patiently.

"You're funny, Pete," I said. "Did you know that Legion Stadium hosted the wrestling matches for the 1932 Olympics? Uncle Charlie told me about them."

"I heard that, too," said Pete. "Hawk said that on dance nights the parking lot fills up with low riders and cool cars. Low riders have their suspension springs changed or sand bags piled in their trunks to lower their chassis. He also said they have pin-striping on their paint jobs and chrome spinners for hub caps. Some cars have whitewall tires like on his car."

VROOM. VROOM. VROOM. "Gotta go 'cause Hawk just fired up his engine and his whitewalls are ready to agitate the gravel," said Pete as he hopped off the swing and ran to the gate. "See ya later, gator."

"After while, crocodile," I called out to Pete's disappearing back then glanced at Buddy. "Hi, Boy. Give me the stick, and I'll throw it while I wait."

The little kids ran around in their good clothes while I threw the stick for Buddy. Uncle Charlie and Aunt Ruthie waved us to their car for the trip to Legion Stadium and the annual Community Children's Christmas Party.

I patted Buddy's head and said, "You be good, and watch the place like a real guard dog." Buddy wagged his tail and answered with a bark.

Uncle Charlie maneuvered his car out of the neighborhood on this crisp and clear afternoon. At the corner of Valley Boulevard and Ramona Boulevard, in downtown El Monte, my uncle turned into the stadium's packed parking lot.

The gray-colored, concrete building was shaped like an "L" lying on its back. The bottom of the "L" soared a hundred feet into the air and had LEGION STADIUM written in block letters across the top. The cars in the parking lot looked like toy cars next to its concrete sides. I watched people streaming into several doorways. They looked like ants.

"Like crazy, like wow! Look at that big building!" I said.

Uncle Charlie parked his car then got out to help Aunt Ruthie. Her beautiful, white, winter coat covered a silky, red dress. A poinsettia brooch sparkled from its spot on her coat's lapel. Rhinestone clips pulled back her auburn hair. *Dad's sister is the most beautiful doctor ever.*

I helped the youngsters out of the car, and we paraded to the entrance of the big building along with other community families. Our family looked fancy in our dress-up clothes. I fingered pearl buttons on my white sweater.

"This is so exciting," I said to the kids as I herded them like sheep. I tucked my purse into the crook of my arm and smoothed out the fingers on my white gloves.

Gail watched me as we walked and asked, "Can you fix my globs, Carol Ann?"

I looked down at Gail's "globs" and stifled a laugh. "Sure I can."

Aunt Ruthie said, "Thank you, Carol Ann, for taking care of the girls' gloves. It's a bit of an art to get all five fingers in the right places."

"That's for sure," I said. "But I'm glad to help them."

At the entrance, Uncle Charlie said, "Stay close so no one gets lost. Inside the cavernous building, it had been transformed into a winter wonderland with beautifully decorated Christmas trees situated around the room. Garlands of snowflakes draped overhead while silver bells and bows adorned the walls. White lights illuminated the entire gigantic interior.

Families sat at tables that had been draped in long, white tablecloths and topped with evergreen and silver centerpieces. Refreshments, and huge punchbowls brimming with sparkling liquid, sat on long tables covered in the same white tablecloths. On stage, a band played soft Christmas music while kids lined up to meet Santa Claus.

"Hey, Carol Ann, sit by us," Pete called out. "Here's an empty table."

"Pete's got a table for us, Uncle Charlie," I said and pointed. "He's over there." So we went "over there" and sat at the saved table.

"This is lovely," said my aunt. "Thank you, Pete, for saving a table."

"You're welcome, Dr. Ruth," said Pete. "Mom told me to save a spot for you while she went to stand in Santa's line with Mandy. May Carol Ann sit at my table?"

"Of course," said Aunt Ruthie then she turned to the little kids. "Who wants to see Santa Claus? Are you taking them, Charlie, or am I?"

Uncle Charlie said, "I'll stay here and hold down the fort, Ruth."

My aunt draped her coat over a chair then took the kids to the line of community kids waiting for Santa. Uncle Charlie turned towards the stage to listen to the band. Excited youngsters ran between the tables. Several of our school friends passed by holding bags of candy.

Pete leaned over and said, "Glad you could make the scene. We got here when the musical program started at noon. Mary Jane got good ideas."

"I bet we'll get a ton of production ideas from this party," I said. "I'm glad our space isn't this big. The hospital party's in a giant-sized space, too."

Hawk turned to me and asked, "Are you going to a Christmas party in the room with the huge window at the top of Los Angeles County Hospital?"

"We're going there next, and Pete gets to go with us," I said.

Hawk said, "If you talk to Santa, ask him to bring me a car radio."

"Get in the line over there, and ask him yourself," laughed Pete. "I can't promise you a new car radio, but I'll bring you a treat from the party."

I said, "Speaking of treats, let's get a candy bag."

After an exciting afternoon, we said good-bye to Pete's family and left. Uncle Charlie led the way, with a supporting hand under Aunt Ruthie's elbow. "That was a fabulous party, and the refreshments were delicious," said my uncle as he steered us across the parking lot.

Inside the car, we settled back for the thirty-minute ride to Los Angeles. Pete said, "This is cool of your aunt and uncle to take me along to their hospital party."

"They like you 'cause you're so well-mannered," I said with a smirk.

"The party we just left was a kick," said Pete as he hefted up his bag of candy. "Mandy almost didn't get in line to see Santa 'cause she saw his elves and was worried she'd see Jack Pumpkinhead from Santa's Village."

"That's so sad that she remembered that scary-looking guy," I said. "He's probably a nice person, but his costume even scared me."

Pete pointed and asked, "Is that the county hospital way out there?"

I nodded my head and answered, "That's it. The hospital is huge inside. The hallways are like train tunnels. Thousands of people work there, and they treat thousands of patients every year. That's the place where my aunt and uncle did their internship in pathology. Now, they're full-fledged doctors of pathology and they work there."

The hospital's Art Deco design stood out clearly the closer Uncle Charlie drove his tank to it. When he pulled into his reserved parking spot, the song, "Up on the Housetop," by Gene Autry, played on the radio. *Soon, we'll be sort of on the hospital's housetop.*

As we emerged from the Plymouth, I looked up the stone walls of the huge hospital towering over us like a giant, white castle. I nudged Pete and pointed, because the city noises and honking cars made it hard to hear.

"We made it, Kiddos," said my uncle as he directed us through a side entrance. The clicking sound of Aunt Ruthie's high heels echoed inside the long corridor. We waited at a bank of elevators until we heard a *ding.* Like a monstrous mouth, the doors slid open in a grin, and the elevator whisked us up twenty floors. It stopped to let us out.

As we moved away from the elevator, Gail looked back and said, "I didn't like riding in the big sliding mouff that gobbled us then threw us up."

Kathleen said, "That was an elevator with a door, Gail, not a mouth."

Pete and I looked the other way so Gail wouldn't see our grins. Uncle Charlie led us into an enormous room that I remembered from last year and the year before. A twenty-foot, decorated Christmas tree formed the centerpiece for the space. It stood in front of the tall window near the top of the building that we had seen from outside.

"Wow!" said Pete. "This is a giant's room and that's a giant's tree."

Aunt Ruthie said, "Charlie, find a table then we'll get our food."

Christmas music filled the room as did hundreds of people. They reminded me of the different colors, shapes, and sizes of the ornaments on the giant Christmas tree. *And each one is beautiful in its own way.* All evening, people greeted my aunt and uncle as we stood in lines and when we sat at our table.

After an evening of fun, food, and gifts, we left the second party of the day for the ride home to El Monte. Back in the car, the little kids nodded off like they did on our ride back from Christmas Tree Lane. I watched the bright city lights of Los Angeles flash by the car windows.

"Two Christmas parties today were coolsville," said Pete with a smile.

I agreed then thought, *Will our Cool Christmas Pageant be coolsville . . . or failuresville?*

9

Trouble on Stage

"What else can go wrong?" screamed Mary Jane as Pete and I entered the tent for rehearsal. Pete's sister stood on the stage holding her hands on top of her blonde hair. *She looks like she's going to pull her hair out,* I thought. *There's trouble on stage.*

"What's the problem, Sis?" asked Pete as he approached her and looked up. Debbie and Mr. Chester's grandson, Oliver, stood nearby.

Mary Jane pointed to Oliver and said, "He's the problem! He broke his arm. Now he can't be 'Snake' in Carol Ann's play." Oliver held up his casted arm.

"I didn't break it on purpose," whined Oliver. "It was an accident."

"Well, your accident is now my headache," complained Mary Jane as she eyeballed Pete. "It's your friend's play, so you can be Snake in the stable."

"Cool it, Sis. I'm not doing that speaking part," said Pete. "I'm helping Hawk's friend, Butch, and his crew from The Cruiser's Car Club move sets and stuff around behind the scenes. I'll be laying a patch outta here if you make me take a part. Sorry."

"That's okay, Pete," I said. "Someone will want to be Snake and slither across the stage hisss-ing out his words." *Last summer, we thought Butch was a snake of a guy until we found out differently.*

"I'll do it," yelled a voice from behind us. Neil emerged from the shadows. "I can still sing with Angela, change costumes, and slither around as Sssnake. Or Oliver can take my place as Joseph in Carol Ann's play."

"You play snake, and Oliver will be Joseph. He can hide his cast under his costume," said Mary Jane as she checked her clipboard. "That change won't affect the programs Dad had printed for us. That's settled, so let's get back to work." She shouted, "BACK TO WORK, EVERYONE!"

Buddy jumped up and scrambled in a circle like a hard worker chasing his tail. I bent down to his beady eye level and said, "She doesn't mean you, Buddy." He tipped his head and snorted.

Pete said, "You can work with me, Buddy, as I move chairs around."

The morning fog rolled in through several tent openings. *It's supposed to be foggy with highs in the 60s all week.* Kids scrambled up and down the stage steps. Hawk's friend, Butch, moved the spotlights into a better position while the song, "Twelve Days of Christmas," played on Mary Jane's record player for the Cool Kid's Choir.

I looked at the program for our Cool Christmas Pageant. A drawing of holly and ribbons framed the pageant title printed across the top of the paper. All our performances were listed down the page. *Mary Jane did a nice job on this.*

The choir that practiced right now was listed near the top of the performances after Mary Jane's introduction and the Parade of Characters. "The Christmas Song" was listed with my dad's name as the singer.

"Are ya writing a book, Carol Ann?" asked Pete. "Can I see it?"

I handed Pete the program as he dropped into the folding chair next to me. "I'm not writing anything. I'm looking at the program that Mary Jane had printed up. She's got everyone and everything in order."

Pete looked the paper up and down and said, "Sis does have a way with words and people. Unfortunately, lots of times she's like a wild woman . . . girl . . .I mean."

"Her wild frown lines mean she's not having fun today," I said.

"She's almost to my play in the program. I hope Neil likes his new part as the sssnake in the stable."

"Better him than me," said Pete as he bounced out of his chair.

I popped out of my chair and joined the other cast members on the stage. We practiced our parts for the pageant. I read my lines as the narrator, while Snake hissed his lines, and the kids made animal sounds.

"Good job," said Mary Jane as she motioned for us to quickly leave the stage. "Oh, by the way, everyone, yesterday we turned in over two hundred dollars to the Community Chest, so they can help needy families here in El Monte. Give yourselves a hand for working really hard selling baked goods and tickets." We clapped our hands.

Buddy howled a long, high-pitched sound to congratulate everyone. Mary Jane frowned down at him. He slunk away to hide under a chair.

Pete whispered, "Mom heard they're giving out three hundred baskets."

From the stage, Mary Jane waved her clipboard and yelled, "Has anyone seen Hawk and his friends? They need to rehearse their spoof of *A Christmas Carol*."

"They disappeared again," Pete said to his sister. "Hawk fired up his hot rod, popped the clutch, and punched his car up and outta the driveway. Hawk's Ride screamed . . . as it tore up the street." *Oops, Mary Jane looks like she's gonna scream.*

"Do you think Hawk and the boys have new girlfriends?" I asked Pete in a soft voice.

"I already thought of that," said Pete. "But Hawk likes that girl from Huntington Beach we met last summer. He's too earthbound . . . too reliable . . . to break her heart. But he's breaking the record for sneaking around with Tim and Ernie."

"Maybe they're Christmas shopping or working side jobs," I said.

"Yeah, maybe," said Pete. "But they're acting . . . kooky."

Mary Jane shouted at several kids which got our attention. We briskly moved around and straightened out folding chairs to look like we were busy. I kept glancing over my shoulder as I moved row after row of chairs. The kids on stage reminded me of a wild swarm of hornets moving every which way.

Pete noticed, too, and said, "That stage looks wild. I told you this is a wild winter. The weather has been wild, we're keeping clues about wild crooks, this is a wild rehearsal today, and its winter . . . a wild winter."

"If you say so, Pete," I said as I picked up trash. "It won't really be winter officially for two more days. I hope all this wild stuff you see turns into a pageant performed on a mild, fog-free evening . . . not a wild, foggy, or rainy one."

Buddy followed me over to the trash can that buzzed with flies. *Yuk.* My doggy circled the trash can sniffing for clues of something ripe to eat.

"That trash stinks like something expired in it," said Pete.

As we hurried inside the tent, I said, "We need to sniff like a hound dog for clues and find out who's stealing from us. We also need to find out where Hawk's going?"

"Righto," said Pete. "The crooks need to get caught and in a hurry. And Hawk needs to hurry and finish what he's doing so we don't have to worry about him."

From the stage, Mary Jane yelled, "Where's Carol Ann?" *Yikes.*

■　　■　　■

Hours of rehearsal later, as the sun set in the west, Pete, Buddy, and I escorted our neighborhood friends to their homes. Buddy needed to run, and we needed to escape from the demon director named Mary Jane. First we dropped Nan and Lindy Chavez off at their home across the street.

In the half-light before dark, shining, multi-colored outdoor lights outlined their roofline. The bay window, on the front of their house, showcased their lighted Christmas tree. A Christmas wreath jingled on the front door as the girls opened the door and disappeared through it.

As we departed for Stu's house, I said, "I'm glad both girls are in my play. Nan makes cool cow noises and Lindy can *baaa* like a lamb."

Pete asked, "What do you think of Neil as a snake?"

"I think he's got the hissing down perfectly," I said. "He learned all his lines really fast, too. He's great as Sssnake."

"I think so, too," said Stu as we moved up his sidewalk to his front door. Colorful ornaments hung from each square in the modern-looking, decorative feature that encased his porch. "See ya tomorrow."

The Bailey boys cut out and raced ahead of us with Buddy hot on their heels. Pete said, "They've got heels on fire. They're in a hurry 'cause they're hungry. There's nothing good on TV tonight unless those brothers like Dinah Shore or Red Skelton."

"Red Skelton will be playing at our house on Dad's RCA Color TV," I said. "After that, Mom's watching *It's a Wonderful Life* with the movie star Jimmy Stewart." I looked up and noticed sparkly stars overhead in the night sky.

"I like watching the stars on TV," said Pete as he glanced up and pointed. "But I really like looking at *those* stars up in God's night sky."

"I love God's stars, too," I said. "Good thing we *split* from the tent an hour ago to have a cookie snack at my house. That way Mary Jane can't blame us for that raunchy, red sucker dangling from the back of her jeans."

"We split just in time," said Pete. "Rehearsals were almost done anyway. She's had a long time to discover the sticky passenger she picked up off of her personal, pink, canvas director's chair."

Pete pulled out his flashlight to light our way. I said, "I wonder if Neil uses the flashlight he got from you. Since rehearsals are done now, the tent will be dark inside. Can you plug in the lights or use your flashlight to light the way inside and get the program I left? I want to show it to my dad."

"Sure," said Pete as we went down his driveway to the dark tent. We followed the flashlighted path into the darker interior. Buddy looked at the stage and barked madly.

Pete swung the flashlight beam to the stage area. We both gasped. Destruction reigned on stage. Buddy rushed up the steps barking furiously and frantically. The slashed stage curtains hung in tatters from broken poles. Their fabric waved eerily in the wind like ghostly arms. Most of the backstage drapes lay on the ground in dark piles.

On the stage steps, Pete grabbed my arm to stop me. The light beam from his flashlight spread across the stage floor that now looked like Swiss cheese. "Don't go any further, Carol Ann. It's not safe," cautioned Pete. "Get back here, Buddy."

"Who did this?" I cried out then buried my face in my hands to sob with shaking shoulders. Buddy whimpered at my feet. I lifted my face and said, "We've worked so hard! Someone pounded holes in the stage floor and slashed our curtains. Why?"

"I don't know why someone did this, but we'll find out!" said Pete as he lit up the stage's corner. "It looks like they found our ticket money hidden under the stage floor over there. Back up, and let's get help."

As we dashed to Pete's back door, I said, "Neil is playing a snake in the stable, but tonight there's a real, snake-type crook who wrecked our stable, stage, and pageant!"

Buddy howled with a long, doleful cry in total agreement with me.

■   ■   ■

Once our parents, neighbors, and Uncle Charlie had assembled in the lighted tent, they assessed the damage. I could tell by their faces that things didn't look good for our pageant. *What are we going to do? We'll have to give back all the ticket money!*

"Who wrecked my stage and special chair?" wailed Mary Jane.

Uncle Charlie took charge and said, "I'm sorry this happened, Kids, but let me call Pastor Myers at Trinity Church and ask him if their fellowship hall is available for you to use this Friday night."

Pete said, "We'll call our friends and family members to tell them about a change of place . . . if we can find one. Then we need to find the crook or crooks who did this."

Mary Jane sat down with a plop on the stage steps and moaned, "How can the show go on?"

"Now Mary Jane has real trouble on stage," whispered Pete as we slipped into the night that mirrored our dark feelings. "What *will* we do?"

"We're going to pray and ask God to help us," I said as I motioned Buddy to me. "Then we're going to believe that the joy of the LORD is our strength like the Bible tells us."

"Okay, Carol Ann," said Pete as he turned toward home. "See ya later, alligator."

"After while, crocodile," I said as a crocodile tear ran down my cheek. Screeching sounded behind the chicken car. *Yikes.* Buddy whimpered as he led the way on the sidewalk to the front porch. *Where are the destroyer crooks now? Are they hanging out in my yard?*

O God, help us please, I prayed as Buddy raced me to our wreath-decorated front door. *Is Adam a destroyer crook?*

10

Snakes in the Stable

THE COOL CHRISTMAS PAGEANT HAS MOVED, said the lettering on the giant, two-way sign set up in front of Pete's house to direct people to the pageant's new location. The rest of the sign's lettering gave the address and directions to Trinity Church located two blocks away on Hemlock Street.

Pete finished attaching the shop lights to the top of the sign and said, "Folks can read this sign and get their directions even after dark." Buddy barked then sniffed around it.

"That's a smart idea, Pete," I said. "You've got some jets, too."

Pete smiled at my compliment about his brains and said, "Thanks, Carol Ann. I'm just doing my job as a grip . . . a guy who works *behind the scenes* with the equipment."

"I'm nervous about being *in front* of the scenes tonight at the pageant," I admitted. "I'm glad to be the narrator for my play so I can *read* from my script. Another good thing is that Buddy's not nervous about playing his part as a barking dog." Buddy woofed out a "yes."

"No sweat," said Pete. "As the narrator, you've got it made in the shade. And Buddy is hip as a barking dog. The play you wrote is cool and so are the costumes."

"Our moms worked really hard on *all* the kids' costumes," I said. "My mouse costume is the cutest and so is Mandy's piglet outfit. Neil's mom made his rattlesnake costume look *too* real. He

■ 93 ■

did a good job at practice all week like all the other kids." Buddy barked for some recognition. "You did a good job, too, Buddy."

"Everyone did a boss job even when the whole pageant moved to the church," said Pete. "Dr. Charles got on the horn . . . his telephone . . . and made a call to find a new place for our pageant. Your uncle saved the day like Mighty Mouse in one of his cartoons."

"Has your dad heard from the police about the destruction?" I asked.

"Dad's officer friend will let him know what he finds out," said Pete.

VROOM, VROOM, VROOM, roared Hawk's Ride as it backed down the driveway. Hawk leaned out of the open window and said, "Hop on board for your chariot ride to Trinity Church. Let's get our final dress rehearsal over with."

"Thanks, Hawk," said Pete as we climbed into the back of the shiny, red-orange machine. Tim smiled at us from the front seat. I moved his crutches over to make more room on the back seat.

VROOM. Hawk floored the gas pedal and cut out up the street. "Razzle Dazzle," by Bill Haley and His Comets, played their Hit Parade song on the radio. Hawk said over his shoulder, "Have you kids finished your Christmas shopping?"

Pete said, "No, but Carol Ann's dad is taking us shopping to-morrow morning. We've got the bread we earned all month from our allowances and doing odd jobs like babysitting, mowing lawns, trimming bushes, and lots of other gigs."

"That's real cool," said Hawk. "Sit back, and hold onto your hats."

At the church, Pete said, "Where is everyone going to park tonight?"

Hawk said, "The ticket holders for our pageant will park here in the church lot and along the street. Our folks will park at Cherrylee School for a short walk to the church."

As we climbed out of Hawk's Ride, a Woody station wagon

pulled up by us. Hawk's surfer friend, Cap, from Huntington Beach, leaned out of the window and said, "Hi Guys, we made the scene. We're here to do our *Christmas in a Little Grass Shack* gig."

"Hi, Guys," said Hawk as Cap, Ruler, Ten Man, and Full Bore exited Cap's Woody along with several teenage girls. "Glad you could make it. I can't wait to see your cool Hawaiian-style Christmas performance."

We traveled across the parking lot to the fellowship hall and into bedlam. Mary Jane directed kids on stage, while Butch and The Cruisers moved folding chairs into three groups to create two center aisles and two side aisles. Music swirled around the room.

Pete and I watched Hawk wander away with a Huntington Beach girl. Pete said, "My brother looks pretty cozy with that cute girl. I think she's his girlfriend."

"I agree," I said. "They look like boyfriend and girlfriend. I'll check that off of my Hawk's Mysterious Disappearances List. Do you think he'll take off again today?"

"I hope not," said Pete. "Let's watch Hawk like hawks."

■   ■   ■

Hawk and his friends never left the rehearsal. They stuck to the Huntington Beach teens like tape on a Christmas package. As folks filed into the hall for The Cool Christmas Pageant, the performers lined up in a back hallway for The Parade of Characters at the show's beginning.

When the musical notes of "We Wish You a Merry Christmas" flowed through the hall, Mary Jane led one line of kids while Debbie led the other. The two leaders in their matching, pink, iridescent snowflake costumes sparkled up the aisles to the stage.

We sang along as we marched to the musical beat like Mickey Rooney and Judy Garland did in one of their many movies. *Their movie characters are always trying to earn money by putting on a backyard song and dance show. We're copying them!*

A group of performers lined up in front of the stage and kept singing while "Mary Jane Snowflake" led the Cool Kid's Choir up the steps and onto the stage. When our opening song ended, the choir sang their medley of Christmas favorites while the rest of us split down the middle aisles like the Red Sea and flowed out the doors.

From back inside the hallway, I listened to Mary Jane. She said, "Welcome, everyone, to our Cool Christmas Pageant with proceeds going to the Community Chest of El Monte. Thank you for purchasing tickets for tonight's performance and buying loads of baked goods. Your freezers must be stuffed."

The audience laughed at that truth. Mary Jane finished by saying, "Because of your generosity, we've donated over three hundred dollars to the Community Chest. They've helped organizations all over El Monte. And now . . . let the show begin."

When it was Dad's turn to perform, I snuck into the dark hall and grabbed a front row seat. Pete slipped in beside me. Dad stepped onto the stage while Pete's mom played the opening bars to "The Christmas Song" on the piano.

The spotlight enhanced Dad's tall, dark, and handsome good looks in his suit and tie. His mellow voice sang out, "Chestnuts roasting on an open fire, Jack Frost nipping at your nose . . ." and on he sang until the song ended followed by thunderous applause.

Pete nudged me and said, "Your dad sings like Nat King Cole. I dig his voice."

Adam tapped my shoulder and said, "He's Nat King Cole's rival."

"Thanks, Guys," I said and motioned for them to follow me as Mary Jane and Debbie took the stage to sing "Suzy Snowflake" in their sparkling snowflake costumes. Out in the hall I said, "There are two more performances then it's showtime for us!"

The cast of animal characters for my play called, *A Snake in the Stable,* waited patiently in a classroom. When I entered the room they greeted me with animal sounds as they practiced their parts. They looked so cute except for Neil and his sinister-looking snake costume. *Yikes! His real-looking costume gives me the creeps!*

When the piano music for "O Little Town of Bethlehem" began to play, it was our cue to line up and go quietly onto the stage behind the closed curtains. The animals positioned themselves while Neil lay facedown on Hawk's car creeper we had borrowed. Hawk used it to lie on his back and work underneath cars. Neil's hands propelled him slowly on the stage. He slithered around like a giant rattlesnake. *Creepy.*

Two eight-foot-tall, painted plywood cutouts of Mary and Joseph stood behind us. A giant-sized manger cutout sat between them with a baby's painted plywood arms waving up to heaven.

Angela and Oliver hid behind the Mary and Joseph cutouts. They moved the giant, fake arms up and down bumping and rustling the real straw sticking up. *Their Mary and Joseph costumes looked cute in the parade.*

Out in front of the curtains, Mary Jane announced, "And next in our pageant program we have an original play written by Carol Ann Hartnell and performed for the very first time this evening. Let's give a hand for *A Snake in the Stable.*

The curtains opened and the audience looked up at us as they applauded. *Yikes. O God, please help us to do a great job.* As Mrs. Mouse, the Narrator, I sat on a tall, chrome stool next to a tall, chrome table borrowed from Dan's Diner.

I adjusted the microphone and read, "The Lord Jesus was born in a Bethlehem stable. His mother, Mary, put him in a straw-filled manger. The animals who live in the dim and cozy stable want to welcome the new family. While Mary and Joseph watch the infant, the animals look at them with wonder. They long to do something special for this special child."

Nan, in her Mrs. Cow costume, took her cue, mooed, and said, "Let us sing a song to the baby Jesus. We can sing a special stable song."

"Yes," said all the animals in the stable.

Snake, with Neil inside, slithered toward me in my Mrs. Mouse costume and said, "Creatures-sss can't sss-sing unless-sss you're a sss-snake with a sss-serious hissing song. Only sss-snakes-sss like me can sss-sing."

I read, "The other animals ignore him because Snake is always *sooo* negative and he wants his-sss own way *all* the time."

Bob Bailey as Mr. Bluebird chirped, "Let's make up a song. Chirp, chirp, chirp."

"Marvelous," mooed Mrs. Cow. "Moo, moo, moo."

"Sss-sorry to interrupt you," hissed Snake. "In your cassse, sss-silence is-sss bessst. Ssshhh."

As Mrs. Mouse, I read, "The animals don't pay attention to Snake's negative words and practice their parts for the stable song."

"Moo, woof, baa, chirp, squeak, honk, quack, peep."

Neil as Snake slithered even closer to me. Buddy scooted to where I sat and growled a low *gggrrrr*. Snake's twelve-foot-long, menacing snakeskin body shook its tail as Neil's scary, snaky, hooded eyes glared up at me through the costume's open mouth. *Yikes.*

Adam, in his horse costume, raised his hoof-covered-hands and pawed them at Snake. *Whoa, this scene is not in my play!* Snake turned away, scooted on the car creeper to the other side of the stage and said, "Sss-someone in this-sss sss-stable can't sss-sing."

I read, "The animals ignore Snake once again and practice their stable song anyway." I pointed to the different animals, so the audience could hear their singing voices.

Mandy Pig oinked, "Oink, oink, oink."

Kathleen Cat meowed, "Meow, meow, meow."
Lindy Lamb baaed, "Baa, baa, baa."
Little Charlie Goose honked, "Honk, honk, honk."
Stu Donkey brayed, "Hee-haw, hee-haw, hee-haw."
Gail Baby Chick peeped, "Peep, peep, poop, oops, peep."
Buddy Dog barked, *woof, woof, woof.*
Cousin Cathie Duck quacked, "Quack, quack, quack."
Nan as Mrs. Cow mooed, "Moo, moo, moo."
As Mrs. Mouse I squeaked, "Squeak, squeak, squeak." I read, "Everyone in this stable can sing. Let everything that has breath praise the LORD. Squeak, squeak."

I continued reading, "Starlight streams into the stable illuminating the baby in the manger. Angelic voices fill the starry night. All the animals look up and see an angel in the distance *flying* over the shepherd's fields."

I glanced up at Edith in her white, flowing angel costume as she sat upon the top of a twelve-foot ladder behind a scene of the shepherd's fields. A spotlight shined on her as she said, "Fear not: for behold, I bring you good tidings of great joy, which shall be to all people. For unto you is born this day a Savior, Christ the Lord." *Yea!* I thought.

I read, "The stable fills with joyous angel voices singing glory to God in the highest. The animals practice their song again with their animal noises." The creatures in their cute costumes, along with Buddy, made their singing sounds.

"Sss-silence, everyone," hissed Snake. "Only I can sss-sing to baby Jesus." Snake slithered toward the manger, turned to the audience, and hissed, "I only want to ta-sss-te the baby's-sss heel with my fangs-sss." The audience gasped loudly. Straw lying on the stage rustled under Snake's scaly "skin" that dragged behind his creeper.

"Stop him," I squeaked as Mrs. Mouse.

"Hold him," hollered Horse as he clomped up and down.

"Chain him," chirped Bob as Mr.Bluebird.

"Block him," baaaa'd Lindy Lamb.

"Hoof him, Horse," honked Goose.

"Pray for help," peeped Gail as Baby Chick.

I read the line, "So the animals bow their heads and pray to God for help."

As Snake crossed into the starlight that flooded down onto the scene near the manger, he stopped and hissed in pain, "Sss-starlight, too bright, no sss-sight! I sss-seek the night." Snake slithered out of the stable scene and into the wings. His long, scaly tail took a long time to leave the stage. *Yikes.*

I read one of the last paragraphs in my play. "The animals cheer that Snake is gone and baby Jesus is safe. They gather close to the manger to sing their stable song. In people language it sounds like the following."

The costumed creatures sang,

"Away in the manger, no crib for His bed,
The little Lord Jesus lay down His sweet head.
The stars in the sky looked down where He lay.
The little Lord Jesus, asleep on the hay."

They continued singing all the stanzas in the song.

I read the final paragraph in my play. "Mary and Joseph smile at the animal sounds. The stable song is sweet music to their ears. The animals agree that Snake is no longer welcome in the stable. The end."

The audience clapped with gusto as the animals, Angela, Oliver, and I proceeded to the front of the stage. Snake slithered out and stood up off of his creeper. The whole cast of *A Snake in the Stable* bowed to the still-clapping audience. Mrs. Rose smiled up at me from her front-row seat. Over in the wings, Pete gave me the thumbs-up sign.

The cast and I left the stage. As we slipped quietly down the hallway, I heard Adam singing, "Hark! The Herald Angels Sing." *Adam just can't be our crook!* Parents waited along the outdoor hall and snapped pictures of their adorable "animal" creatures that were my cast members.

Pete caught up with me and said, "Congratulations, Carol Ann. You're play was cookin'! It was really boss. And Neil made a seriously, sinister snake!"

"Thanks, Pete," I said. "It was scary to look at Neil as Snake and at all those people in the audience, but God helped me 'cause he gave me his joy and strength."

"I heard Buddy growl at Neil," said Pete as he bent down and patted Buddy's head. "You were a good doggy to protect Carol Ann from Snake."

I said, "Wait, while I put my creatures with their parents, so we can watch the rest of the pageant. I want to see Hawk's *Three Scrooges* skit."

After a few minutes, Pete and I found seats in the hall and watched the end of the funny Hawaiian Christmas skit by the beach teens. "They fracture me," said Pete. "I'm glad they're our friends."

"They were funny," I said and looked down at my program. "Our school friends are next and then "The Drummer Boy." Hawk's skit ends the pageant. What a kick it will be."

Becky, Susan, and Eileen, from our sixth-grade class at Cherrylee School, paraded onto the stage. They wore silky tunics with crowns on their heads and lots of fake jewels around their necks. One of them held a treasure chest while the others carried gold flasks. Mrs. Hawking played the piano as the girls sang, "We Three Kings."

After a fine drum performance of "The Drummer Boy" by a

local teenage boy, Hawk, Ernie, and Tim performed their skit called *The Three Scrooges*. Their performance was a spoof on Charles Dickens's famous book, *A Christmas Carol*. We laughed at their animated antics.

When the three teens had finished most of their skit, Tim switched to the part of Tiny Tim from *A Christmas Carol*. The audience sighed for Tim's real struggle across the stage with his well-worn crutches. *How can we help Tim learn to walk without crutches? Can more therapy help? Please, God, do a miracle in Tim's life.*

Tim looked out at the audience and said those famous words of Tiny Tim, "God bless you, everyone, and a Merry Christmas to one and all."

Hawk and Ernie stood on each side of Tim as each of them took a bow while the audience clapped. As they straightened up, Hawk said, "We'd like to thank everyone for making this a very special night. We especially want to thank Mr. Chester for his contributions to the pageant and to a miracle in this season of giving."

Pete said, "It sure is a miracle that we produced this *unreal* pageant."

Before I could answer him, Tim handed his crutches to Hawk and Ernie then very slowly stepped forward on the stage. He carefully stepped back then shuffled in a circle.

Tim turned to the audience and said, "I want to thank you, Mr. Chester, for paying my daily therapy bills. The miracle of therapy has given me back my legs. But more importantly, the miracle of your giving has given me hope for my future. Teenage Tim can walk without a crutch! Merry Christmas, everyone, and thank you."

The audience erupted into a standing ovation like a wave rising out of the sea. Salty tears coursed down faces near me as twin trails of tears coursed down my face like miniature rivers. Pete wiped at his nose. Mrs. Hawking once again played "We

Wish You a Merry Christmas" on the piano as people left the hall with smiling faces.

Pete sniffed and said, "Well, we've solved the mystery that drove us wild all month. We now know the details of Hawk's disappearing act! But we still need to discover the snakes in our stable."

I glanced at Pete as we went to find our folks. I said with a shudder, "Are their *real* snakes in our stable? What stable are you talking about? We don't *have* a stable!"

"Dad's officer friend said they found two sets of footprints leading up to and away from our tent stage . . . our "stable" when the scenery was in it. That means we're looking for two crafty crooks . . . two snakes in the stable."

"It's going to take another miracle to find them even with all our clues," I said. "The only miracle I want to think about tonight is Tim's miracle of walking! That's the best Christmas gift any of us could ever get . . . to see a friend made whole! And to know it happened because of another friend's generosity."

Pete said, "Tonight we learned about giving and Christmas miracles."

"We sure did," I said and Buddy agreed with a happy howl. *But can we get one more miracle? Can our clues catch the crooks before they hurt us again?*

Christmas Eve Excitement

"Last night's pageant was wild!" said Pete as he gobbled up a piece of my mom's coffee cake. "It was boss that Mr. Chester paid money so Tim can walk without his crutches."

"It's a miracle," I said as I took a bite of coffee cake. "It's our very own *Christmas Carol* story. I bet lots of folks at church tonight will still be thinking about it during our special Christmas program. Miss East is leading our Children's Choir in singing Christmas songs. Is your family going to church tonight?"

"Yeah, my family is going to a Christmas Eve Service at our church," said Pete as Mom entered her kitchen. "Mrs. H, this is the best coffee cake!"

"Thanks, young man. Now scoot," said Mom. "The kids are waiting."

"Let's go, Pete," I said as I looked outside at the patio. "See ya out front, Buddy."

As Pete and I scooted up the sidewalk to Dad's car and the waiting kids, Buddy's feet pattered to catch up with us. Then the little hound raced ahead and circled us like a spinning top before running back behind our house.

Dad smiled as we climbed into the backseat of Mom's Hudson Jet automobile for our Christmas Eve shopping spree. I patted my purse containing my shopping money.

"Are you ready to shop?" asked Dad as he started the car and cruised up the driveway on his way out of the neighborhood. "Who wants to visit Santa Claus?"

The little kids shouted, "We do!"

"We don't," I said. "Pete has a long list of gifts to get, and so do I."

Dad said, "That's fine. The winter coat I bought for your mom is on hold at the department store. I'll keep the little kids with me while you go shopping."

"Thanks, Dad," I said. "Be sure and take them along the sidewalk to see all the Christmas window displays for some Christmas Eve excitement."

"Thanks for taking me today, Mr. H," said Pete. "You sang like a pro last night."

"Thanks, Pete," said Dad and began to sing, "Chestnuts roasting on an open fire."

In downtown El Monte, Christmas decorations adorned every square inch of every window, door, and counter in every store. Shoppers bustled by us with smiles and frowns. Pete and I joined the bag-carrying throng of folks on the downtown sidewalks.

The Christmas song, "Silver Bells," played while the same smiling Salvation Army lady rang her "silver" bell for donations.

"Let's put some money in her red pot," I said to Pete and dropped in a few coins.

Pete agreed, dropped in two dimes, and said, "Let's duck into the drugstore. They've got everything for a "last minute Santa" like me."

We slipped into the drugstore filled with Christmas gifts and decorations. I said, "Okay, last minute Santa, I need to look at the boxed jewelry sets that were advertised in the newspaper."

After a busy and productive hour of shopping, we met Dad back at Mom's car. Everyone carried bags as we climbed inside. Gail smiled and said, "We got Mommy some cologner."

Kathleen corrected Gail, "We got cologne for Mommy, not cologner."

"I'm sure she'll love it, Girls," I said as I patted my shopping bags. "I bought Mom lovely jewelry and cool presents for you kids. But they're a surprise."

As Dad drove through traffic, Pete said, "I got my dad a full pound of nuts in the shell for forty-nine cents. Plus, I found boss stuff for everyone else. I had enough bread to buy the gifts I needed. The drugstore had a top cowhide fielder's glove with rawhide lacing for only two dollars and ninety-eight cents. I hope Santa brings me one of those."

From the front seat, Dad said, "It's a good thing the fog lifted before your pageant and that we didn't get the rain the Weather Bureau predicted. Up north, they're getting flood-producing rains for the wildest winter weather they've had in fifteen years."

Pete glanced at me and said, "I told Carol Ann this is a wild winter."

"I know," I said as I rolled my eyes. "Our Cool Christmas Pageant was a kick. I was scared to narrate my play, but I knew the joy of the LORD was my strength."

Dad said, "I'm real proud of you, Carol Ann, and your sisters. The newspaper from yesterday was full of articles about youth groups performing at their churches."

Gail said, "I messted up my peep last night." Kathleen rolled her eyes.

The song, "There's No Place Like Home for the Holidays," played on the car's radio. Back on our driveway, Buddy greeted us with his wagging tail as we exited the car. He followed us up the sidewalk to our house. *Even Buddy knows there's no place like home for the holidays.* Pete and I went inside and dropped our purchases in the den.

"I'll get the paper, ribbon, and tags to wrap our gifts," I said.

"That's hip, Carol Ann, 'cause I can't wrap presents," said Pete as he turned on our black and white TV in the corner. He sat on the scratchy, gray sofa and looked through the TV-DIAL-O-LOGUE. "Let's watch the end of *Tales of the Texas Rangers*."

We spent the early afternoon watching the end of *Texas Rangers*, all of *The Bishop's Wife*, and wrapping presents. Delicious baking smells wafted to us from the kitchen, so Mom let us sample a few cookies. As gold and purple streaks painted the sunset sky, I escorted Pete to his house. Mary Jane waited for him at the gate.

For once, Mary Jane smiled as she said, "You did a good job last night, Carol Ann. I was surprised. You narrated your play with no mistakes."

"Aw gee, Sis, Carol Ann was flat-out, in orbit last night," said Pete. "She was in the know and did a boss job in front of the audience."

"If you say so," said Mary Jane with a smirk. "Mom wants you home for dinner, so we can leave for the Christmas Eve service at church."

"I'll be right in," said Pete as Mary Jane stomped off to their house. "She's my sister and I love her, but she's gotta stop putting you down."

"It's okay, Pete," I said with a smile. "She can't steal my special Christmas joy. But I do hope we can find the crooks who stole our money."

"The Heat . . . I mean police are talking to our backyard neighbor, Mrs. Green," said Pete. "She called the police when she noticed suspicious footprints across the goose goop in her backyard and piled up crates in the fence corner. Did Adam leave prints?"

I got my notepad. "I hope not, but it is physical evidence."

"Yeah," said Pete as pounding sounds vibrated across his backyard. "That's my dad and Hawk nailing plywood over the holes on the stage, so we can still use it."

"I'm glad they can salvage the stage," I said.

"Dad said someone was real mad to do that," said Pete. "But this mystery will have to get solved after Christmas. I'll see you at your aunt's house when we get home."

"Okay. And we're not serving Eggnog Pie or Mincemeat Mold!" I said and waved goodbye to Pete as he sprinted away.

I looked at the list in my notepad: thefts from school and names including the janitor, missing money from bake sale, missing money from our hiding place under the stage, footprints in the goose goop in Mrs. Green's backyard, plus the crates piled up at her fence. *Can the police solve this mystery? O God, help them, please,* I prayed.

■ ■ ■

During the Christmas Eve service at our church that night, Rev. Myers preached an inspired message then read the Christmas story from Luke 2:1-11.

He read, "'And it came to pass in those days, that there went out a decree from Caesar Augustus, that all the world should be taxed . . . And all went to be taxed, every one into his own city. And Joseph also went up from Galilee . . . To be taxed with Mary his espoused wife, being great with child. And so it was, that, while they were there . . . she brought forth her firstborn son, and wrapped him in swaddling clothes, and laid him in a manger; because there was no room for them in the inn.'"

Gail whispered to me, "What's a swaddle and did it hurt the baby?"

I tried not to laugh and said, "Mary gently wrapped up baby Jesus."

Rev. Myers finished reading the story,

"'And there were in the same country shepherds abiding in the field . . . And, lo, the angel of the Lord came upon them, and the glory of the Lord shone round about them: and they were sore afraid. And the angel said unto them, Fear not: for, behold, I bring you good tidings of great joy, which shall be to all people. For unto you is born this day in the city of David a Saviour, which is Christ the Lord.' Amen and Merry Christmas to all."

I love that joy word!

The choir sang, "O Holy Night." I read the words carved in wood above their heads. "Be still, and know that I am God." Psalm 46:10.

The smiling congregation filed out of the church pews, up the aisles, and into the chilly night. People greeted one another and wished each other "Merry Christmas."

Uncle Charlie said, "That was a fabulous service. Let's go home and have dessert, Kiddos, so we can tuck you into bed before Santa arrives." The youngsters squealed in delight like piglets in a merry mud puddle.

Back at my aunt and uncle's house, we enjoyed a dessert buffet bash laid out in Aunt Ruthie's kitchen. Someone pounded on the back door, so I opened it. Pete stepped into the warm kitchen holding a present. He eyeballed the delicious desserts spread out across the table.

"What's buzzin, cuzzin?" asked Pete as he glanced around the room then handed Aunt Ruthie the gift. "Mom sent me over to give you this. She hopes you like it."

"Thank you," said Aunt Ruthie with a smile. "I'm sure I will."

Pete moved near me. I said, "Grab a plate and get some goodies."

"Thanks, Carol Ann," said Pete. "I believe I will. Then you need to walk over to my house for the special Christmas treats that Mom baked up from your mom's recipes."

After eating all the goodies on our loaded plates, Pete and I went outside and through the gate into his yard. Buddy bounded in front of us like he led the way. The tall, white tent in Pete's yard looked ghostly with the quarter moon shining on it. *Did the police miss any evidence that might still be in the tent?*

"Pete . . . eee!" yelled Mary Jane. "Mom needs you!"

"I'll be right there!" Pete yelled back to her. "Wait here, Carol Ann, and let Buddy protect you. I'll be right back, so I can show you the new stage floor inside the tent."

As Pete charged to his back porch, Buddy charged over to the tent and started frenzied barking and howling. He darted through the opening and disappeared. *Yikes.* I crept slowly to the tent's open flap and peeked inside.

This kind of Christmas Eve excitement is not exciting! It's scary! Da dump pounded my heart. *Where's Buddy? Where's Pete to help me?*

One light bulb, hanging from the ceiling, illuminated part of the tent. Buddy barked frantically behind the stage. Then he raced in and out of the shadows next to the stage. The shadows looked like long, dark fingers. I shivered in the cold Christmas Eve night air.

"Here, Buddy," I whispered, but he ignored me as he charged around.

Above him dangled the sagging curtains on the last of the boards to be removed. *What's that over there on the grass next to the stage?* I inched forward, bent down, and picked up a flashlight that looked familiar. *Plunk. What's that? Is someone watching me? Yikes!*

Under the remaining curtains, two sparkly shoes stuck out from below the fabric. *I know those shoes! They belong to . . .* "OW!" *What just hit my head? What's happening?* I stumbled to the ground, engulfed in dark swirls of fabric that weighed me down. *I can't breath.* Frantic footsteps tapped in my direction. Buddy howled in the distance as everything turned completely and utterly black . . . then white.

The CLOUD 9 AMUSEMENT PARK banner whipped in the blowing snowflakes above my head. Its Welcome Center looked strangely familiar as I stumbled to it through the snow. A soaring snowball whizzed past my ear and slammed into a snowdrift. The song, "Let it Snow, Let it Snow, Let it Snow," swirled out of a loud speaker.

"I almost hit you, Carol Ann," said Mary Jane from behind me.

I turned to look at her. A snowball plopped on the sleeve of my special Christmas coat. Buddy growled a low guttural noise then barked like crazy.

"Let's go, Buddy," I said as I stepped in the snow behind Buddy, my "doggy" snowplow.

"You can't escape," shouted Mary Jane like a wild woman.

"We can try," I called back to her. "Buddy, let's duck in here."

As we darted into the park's Welcome Center, I realized it looked like the one at Santa's Village but in a 1950s style. An Elvis Santa greeted us, and so did his Rock 'n' Roll Elves. When Jack Pumpkinhead popped into view, Buddy howled in fright.

"Where am I?" I asked a pixie. "This looks like a Rock 'n' Roll Santa's Village."

"It is," said the pixie. "And you can never leave." She looked familiar as she approached me wearing sparkly shoes. Where did I see those shoes before? She said in Angela's voice, "I'm so very sorry you can never leave."

Buddy and I rushed past the park employees and out to the rides. Mary Jane raced behind us throwing more snowballs. She yelled, "Put down, put down, Carol Ann."

Pete yelled to me from a Cloud Car Ride overhead, "Don't listen to her, Carol Ann. I'll be right back when I get off of this cloud ride to nowhere. Wait there, Carol Ann."

"Hurry, Pete," I called to the cloud car zipping away on the park's monorail.

"There'sss no asistance for you," said a monstrous rattlesnake as it slithered towards me. A familiar flashlight rolled near him. His forked tongue twitched at me as he said, "Pete can't sss-save you." Snake rose up and reared back to strike at me.

"Not so fast, Snake," said Mr. Chester as he pounded Snake with his crutch. While Snake backed up, Mr. Chester said, "Run, Carol Ann and Buddy. Go that way!"

We scurried back through the Welcome Center and out into the swirling, twirling, falling snow that turned everything bright white. Bing Crosby's voice sang "White Christmas."

"I'm sorry," echoed behind me.

"Please, God, help us," I called. "This is too much Christmas Eve excitement! I can't see anything!" I raised my arms and batted at the blindingly white, wild, wintry world surrounding me. "Help!"

12

Christmas at the Tent

"Carol Ann, Carol Ann, Carol Ann," called my sisters. My white world opened up when Gail pulled back the sheet. "It's Christmas morning, Carol Ann. Wake up."

"I'm up, Gail," I said as I sat up in my bed and stretched. *Ow, that hurts,* I thought. Christmas morning sunshine streamed through my bedroom windows and past the pink, ruffled curtains.

"Santy Claud left us lots of presents, so get up, Carol Ann," said Gail.

I threw back my covers and felt the floor for my slippers. When I pushed my hair back out of my eyes, I felt a large lump on my head. "Ow, that hurts, too," I said.

Gail watched me and said, "You got bumped out last night. Auntie Ruthie check . . . ted you and told Mommy to watch you in case you had a con. . . . cusster."

Kathleen said, "It's called a concussion, Gail. Pete found you under a pile of curtains that fell down when Angela moved from behind them."

"I help . . . ted you," said Gail. "And so did Buddy. He woofed at that girl."

"Angela kept saying she was sorry over and over," said Kathleen. "Daddy carried you home and put you to bed before Santa Claus got here."

Mom called from the living room, "Hurry up, Girls, so your

dad can get home movies of you walking out here."

Angela hurt me? I finished putting my feet into my new slippers and followed Kathleen and Gail out of my bedroom. Their matching, red flannel nightgowns looked cute. I glanced down and gasped. *I match them . . . we're triplets! Yikes.*

"Smile, Girls, and stand by the tree," said Dad. "Merry Christmas."

Our lighted, decorated Christmas tree glimmered with tinsel and sparkly ornaments. Wrapped presents sat tucked beneath the tree's branches. Goodies filled our four felt stockings and Buddy's mesh stocking hanging on the fake fireplace.

"Open your presents then we'll get dressed and have breakfast," said Mom as we piled our gifts for her onto her lap. She smiled as she opened each thoughtful gift. Mom opened the "Boxed Set" necklace and earrings that I gave her and put them on.

"I'm glad you like the jewelry, Mom," I said. "I picked out the prettiest set."

Gail opened an especially large box and chirped, "I got just what I ben always wanting." She pulled the Bride Dancing Doll out of the box and held her up. The doll was almost as tall as Gail and looked pretty in her white, rayon taffeta bride dress. Gail danced around the living room to the record, "Have Yourself a Merry Little Christmas".

Dad opened his gift from me. "Thanks, Carol Ann. I love the tie."

I smiled at myself in the mirror of the Stardust Dresser Set I had just opened. "This is perfect for my dresser. I'll look in my own mirror when the bathroom's *in use.*"

Kathleen opened The Bobbsey Twins Play Box with two paper dolls and twenty-six colorful costumes. She pulled out an activity book, a coloring book, and a story book. She held up her present and said, "I have my very own paper dolls now. Yea!"

Two-year-old Mark giggled gleefully when Dad sat him on the saddle of a palomino plush horsey with rubber-tired wheels.

Mark grabbed the bridle with one toddler hand and the horse's flowing mane with the other. "Hortey," squealed Mark.

Mom laughed and said, "When you girls are done, tuck your gifts back under the tree and put on your Christmas outfits. We'll have breakfast and later we'll go to the Hawking's Christmas party in the tent."

I whispered, "Thanks, Mom, for the store-bought clothes, jewelry, and books."

An hour later, we enjoyed a buffet breakfast: coffee cake, crispy bacon, scrambled eggs, muffins and orange juice. I brushed crumbs from my blue sweater coat. Buddy ate his dry dog food then scattered his new toys from his doggy stocking around the patio.

I cracked the back door open and kneeled down to look in Buddy's beady, black eyes. "Happy Birthday, Buddy," I said. He dropped down, rolled over, and kicked his legs.

Loud knocking on our front door caused Buddy to roll over, jump up, and bark. Now I jumped up from the floor as Mom opened the door and ushered Pete, Mr. Chester, and Adam's whole family inside.

"Merry Christmas," said Pete as he sniffed like a hound dog through the kitchen and outside onto the patio. "Happy Birthday, Buddy. We've got a surprise for you." Pete picked up the birthday boy and said, "Look at your surprise present, Buddy."

Adam and his dad carried a brand new doghouse through our house and settled it on the patio. Buddy sniffed around the wooden box with a roof. He ducked inside then he peeked out of the rounded opening. Buddy dropped down, put his head on his paws, and barked out a thank-you to Adam and his dad. *Adam looks so innocent. He's too nice to have hurt us.*

"He loves it," I said with a shaky voice that tried not to cry. "He needed a new one. Thank you so much for giving Buddy the best birthday present ever." Buddy howled his agreement.

Adam's family smiled as Adam said, "You're welcome, Carol Ann. But even though we did the labor, it was Mr. Chester's idea to build Buddy a new home."

I looked up at old Mr. Chester, smiled really big, and said, "Thank you so much, Mr. Chester. You're the best neighbor ever!" Then I gave Mr. Chester a great big hug.

He patted my back, looked down at me, and said, "You're welcome. You're both scrappy, and you suit each other."

Everyone laughed as we enjoyed this special moment between neighbors and friends. Mom said, "Please, have a bite of breakfast. We have plenty to share. It will go to waste if you don't help us eat it."

After those encouraging words, everyone dug in with gusto. When Pete finished eating, I followed him to his place to help him decorate for their Christmas party later today.

As we entered the tent, Pete asked, "How's your head, Carol Ann? You really scared me this time. I thought you were a goner."

I put my hand up, touched the lump on my head, and said, "It hurts, but I'm okay. I don't remember being carried home, or going to bed. What happened?"

Pete said, "When I got back to the tent last night, I didn't see you, but I heard Buddy barking. I went inside and saw your shoe sticking out from under the heavy curtains that had fallen on top of you. Angela stood like a statue screaming, 'I'm sorry. I'm so sorry. I didn't mean to hurt Carol Ann. She's under there.' That's when I started praying."

"Right before my world went dark, I found the flashlight you gave Neil," I said. "I picked it up and saw Angela's shoes under the curtain where she was hiding. I don't think she meant to hurt me. When she moved, the curtains must have tumbled down."

"That's what she said as I yelled for help. We pulled boards and curtains off of you. Buddy licked you like crazy, but you were on cloud nine. Dr. Ruth checked you for broken bones. My dad called the police and Angela sang like a snowbird."

"Yikes. I had a horrible nightmare about the CLOUD NINE AMUSEMENT PARK that looked like a 1950s style Santa's Village," I said as I put chairs around a table. "Snake from my play reared up to strike me, but Mr. Chester bonked him."

"What a wild dream," said Pete as we moved to the next table.

"It was wild all right," I said. "Mary Jane lobbed snowballs at me to 'put me down.' I remembered you had called her a wild woman."

Pete laughed and said, "I think you may be one, too, Carol Ann. You wrote down clues for the wild stuff going on all month, found Neil's flashlight which was the physical evidence we needed that pointed to one of the crooks, and disarmed both crooks by getting hurt."

"I didn't do anything great. I was scared to go into the tent last night without you," I said. "But I was more worried about Buddy, so I peeked inside and asked God to give me strength. I needed your KID COURAGEOUS cape right then. Buddy was barking like wild, so I investigated and found the flashlight. I heard a noise and was scared shaky."

While we covered the round tables with red tablecloths, Pete said, "Angela said they only wanted money. When they couldn't get the lock off of our side door in the stage where we hid our cash box, Neil found a sledge hammer and made a hole. Then they grabbed the cash."

"So why didn't they *leave* with the cash?" I asked as we topped the tables with white plates and candy cane cloth napkins. "And why did they wreck the stage that everyone worked so hard to build?" I glanced at Buddy sniffing the restored stage. He looked over at me and tipped his cute, little head. One black ear drooped to the side.

Pete glanced that way, too, and said, "Hawk and Dad finished nailing down the plywood last night. They didn't even have to knock the curtains down 'cause you took care of that."

"Why did Angela and Neil tear up the stage and hurt our pageant?" I asked.

Pete said, "Neil went ape with the sledge hammer and admitted that he was mad at both of us for gathering clues last fall against his best friend. After he made the hole to get the cash box, he kept hitting the stage floor and swinging the sledge hammer at the curtains."

"What was Angela doing?" I asked as I finished putting the last napkin in place.

"She said she begged Neil to stop," said Pete. "She got scared when he went wild. She wanted cash for Christmas shopping since her parents told her to earn her own shopping money. Angela and Neil were our crooks in the classroom, at the bake sale, and on our stage. Not Adam!"

"I'm glad it wasn't Adam," I said. "Angela earned her money all right. That was a lot of hard work to steal from us and the poor people in town. Why did she come back to the scene of the crime?" Buddy howled like he knew the answer to my question.

"She had dropped Neil's flashlight in one of the holes on the stage and knew it was evidence, so she snuck back over here after dark to find it," said Pete. "But Hawk found it when he was working on the stage and tossed it in the grass where *you* found it."

"Angela's sparkly shoes were a clue that gave her away," I said.

"Those shoes left footprints through Mrs. Green's backyard," said Pete. "Her and Neil sneaked across it and climbed the fence into my yard."

"Hopefully, the police would have matched her shoes to those footprints," I said as I set down a pine centerpiece with cookies and lollypops sticking out of it. "Is this centerpiece your idea for the party? It's cool-looking. I get dibs on that large, red-striped lollypop right there."

"Mom had the idea," answered Pete. "We reused the stuff from Dad's company party. I took out the gold ornaments from the original centerpieces, left the red ribbons, then stuck in lolly-pops and cookies on sticks. Mom wanted Christmas at the tent to look like a sweet shop for *my* sweet tooth!"

"You're so cool, Pete," I said as I stepped back to eyeball our handiwork. "And you're cool, too, Buddy." I bent over and ruffled the short, tan fur on the top of his head. Cool Buddy nodded his head up and down.

Each table dressed in its tablecloth and centerpiece made the tent look like a candy shop. Red crepe paper, white balloons, and lights crisscrossed the tent ceiling from corner to corner like giant candy canes. Someone had draped red and white bunting around the stage and set up a decorated Christmas tree.

Pete said, "Aw, gee, this place looks unreal. I'm glad you could make the scene. It's Coolsville for sure like the cool decorations at Dan's Diner. Too bad the diner didn't win the decorating contest."

"I agree," I said. "After last night, I'm glad to make the scene."

"Pete . . . eee!" yelled Mary Jane as she stomped into the tent. "There you are and hey . . . you decorated!" Mary Jane looked around. "It looks cool . . . like a candy shop."

"Thanks, Sis," said Pete. "We aim to please . . . some of the time."

"Well, the decorations look pleasing," she said as she turned to me. "I'm glad to see you're okay, Carol Ann. Without you around, Pete would be under foot all the time, kinda like your mangy, little mongrel over there." Buddy looked up like he understood then he scooted under a folding chair.

As Mary Jane marched away, Pete shook his head and called to her, "Merry Christmas."

"Well, at least she's not slinging snowballs at me like she did in the scary dream I had," I said. "A few cold words are easier to duck, huh, Buddy? Would you like a birthday treat?" Buddy dipped his head sideways and barked out a yes. I handed him a homemade, decorated dog bone treat.

Soon the tent filled up with friends and neighbors. Perry Como sang "There Is No Christmas like a Home Christmas" from his Christmas album that played on Mary Jane's record player. Cookies, cakes, and candy plus regular food filled the table at the buffet bash.

In the buffet line, Pete said, "This party is cookin with my favorite friends and treats. It's cool to see Tim walking with only his braces and without crutches, thanks to Mr. C."

I looked at Mr. Chester who sat at a table with Stu and Adam's family. His crutch leaned against his chair. I said, "Mr. Chester gave Tim the gift of freedom."

Pete said, "Cause Mr. C understands what a gift that is."

"Mr. Chester also gave Adam's family the gift of a new start," I said. "And I'm really glad that Neil and Angela gave Adam the gift of innocence when they confessed."

"Yeah, me too," said Pete. "I never *really* thought Adam was guilty."

"I never did either," I said. "He's been a good friend to us."

We took our loaded dessert plates to an empty table by the stage. Buddy ran ahead of us then scrunched down with his head on his paws. I gave him more homemade birthday treats from my pocket. He sniffed them then crunched them with his sharp teeth.

"Buddy likes his birthday treats," I said. "How are your tasty treats?"

"Like wow! All my favorites are here for my munching mouth," said Pete as he bit into a chocolate chip cookie. "Even though Angela and Neil are bad news, they are sorry. Last night, they turned themselves into the police and confessed to everything they did, which helps their case. I forgive them. Can you forgive them, Carol Ann?"

I looked at Pete and said, "Of course I forgive them, 'cause God forgives me! Besides writing down clues during this wild winter, I wrote a list of giving."

"Read me your list," said Pete as he popped a perfect, powdered-sugar-covered crescent cookie into his mouth.

I took my notepad out of the angora trimmed pocket on my special Christmas coat. I crossed out my clues and flipped the page. With my stubby pencil, I added three more things to my list of ways to give to others all year long and not just at Christmas time.

I read, "Things to give all year: time, money, kind words, compliments, help, joy, encouragement, gentleness, patience, gratitude, friendship, freedom, and forgiveness."

"Wow, Carol Ann," said Pete. "That's a cool list. I hope I can do those things."

"Wait," I said. "There's one more gift, and it's the best gift of all . . . love. We give love because God first loved us and gave his Son, Jesus, to each of us as the Perfect Gift."

Pete nodded his head and said, "He's the coolest gift of all!"

I glanced back down at my notepad and said, "Don't forget our special Bible verse. The end of Nehemiah 8:10 says, 'the joy of the LORD is my strength.'"

"Thanks for reminding me, Carol Ann," answered Pete with a grin as he lifted up his bent arm, flexed his bicep, and tapped the muscle.

On stage, the little kids giggled, got our attention, opened their song books, and announced they would sing the song, "Joy to the World." *Recently, I read about this special song,* I thought. Isaac Watts wrote the lyrics in 1719 from music written by

George Frederick Handel. Sweet voices sang,

"Joy to the World, the Lord is come!
Let earth receive her King;
Let every heart prepare Him room,
And Heaven and nature sing,
And Heaven and nature sing,
And Heaven, and Heaven, and nature sing."

We sang joyfully as Buddy joyfully crunched his birthday doggy biscuits. Our voices soared around the tent and up to heaven.

"Joy to the World, the Savior reigns!
Let men their songs employ;
While fields and floods, rocks, hills, and plains,
Repeat the sounding joy,
Repeat the sounding joy,
Repeat, repeat, the sounding joy."

While everyone sang out the last lines of this classic Christmas carol, Pete leaned in my direction. He whispered, "Hey, Carol Ann, the joy of the Lord is our strength."

"It sure is, just like this song about joy," I answered in a whisper. "Merry Christmas, Pete."

"Merry Christmas, Carol Ann!"

Special Epilogue

Hawk's New Year's Eve Circus Party

"Rock the Joint" filled the tent with loud sounds as Buddy and I slipped inside. Giant, painted plywood circus scenes decorated the tent's canvas walls. Buddy raced to a painting of an open tent flap with painted circus animals outside it against a backdrop of winter hills and starry skies that looked familiar. My dog sniffed, barked, and howled.

I scooted after Buddy as I glanced around and whispered, "Buddy, they're not real animals. You need to be a good puppy at this party and stop howling." I scooped him up into my arms and petted his tan head to calm him down. "And *no* chasing anything!"

"Does your little mongrel have to howl at *everything* he sees?" asked Mary Jane.

Too late, I thought, as I turned to face Pete's sister. She stood in front of me with her arms crossed wearing her sparkly snowflake costume from our Cool Christmas Pageant. One of her black, patent leather shoes tapped out an impatient tune

"I'm sorry, but Buddy only barked at the animals in that scene because he thought they were real. He'll be good," I promised.

"He'd better be, or you're out of here," said Mary Jane in a gruff and vicious voice.

Pete sprinted up to us with his red cape billowing out behind him. He broke the tension that made me feel like a tight-rope acrobat balancing on a thin wire. He said, "Hi, Carol Ann. Hi, Buddy. Way to make the scene. How do you like our circus tent? Tim painted the circus scenes. Aren't they boss?"

"Eveything's so cool," I said. "Thanks for inviting us to Hawk's New Year's Eve Circus Party. I glanced around the entire tent and up to the ceiling. "The red crepe paper and white balloons you draped across the ceiling for your Christmas at the Tent party still look good and they match the circus theme. The bunting on the stage matches, too, minus the tree."

"Aw, the balloons lost air, but we left them up anyway," said Pete.

Mary Jane chimed in with a comment, "Pete, Hawk and I had a decorating day to put up the circus decor. Mom washed the red tablecloths so we could reuse them for this party, and I helped her sew hems on those fabric, clown-print napkins. It was *my* idea to keep the stage decorated."

As Mary Jane talked, we shuffled slowly across the grass to an empty table in the back of the tent by a mural of a lion tamer in a center ring surrounded by wild beasts. From my arms, Buddy growled with a low motor sound at the painted lions and tigers. I put him on the grass, scrunched down to his level, and warned him with a finger to my mouth.

"We've got dibs on this table," said Pete as we circled it and pulled out chairs. The record, "Good Rockin' Tonight," by Elvis Presley, played on Mary Jane's record player that sat on *her* stage.

Pete waved his arms and whirled his red lion tamer, KID COURAGEOUS cape as he said, "There's the rest of our crowd."

Our Cherrylee "crowd" waved then walked in our direction. Stu, Adam, the Bailey brothers, Susan, Becky, Eileen, and Edith approached our corner. The boys looked nice in white shirts tucked into jeans. The girls wore frilly, fancy dresses with sweaters.

Mary Jane moved away while speaking over her shoulder, "See you later, ankle biters and mangy mutt." She hurried to the tent's opening to intercept her snowflake twin, Debbie. Then she motioned to Oliver Chester and Nan, from across the street.

Our school friends pulled out chairs to sit down. Conversations flew back and forth across the red tablecloth-covered table like bags of peanuts tossed into the spectator stands. Pete dipped his hand in a popcorn-filled bowl that formed part of a centerpiece along with a bigger bowl of horns, whistles, and noisemakers. Small bowls on the table held orange marshmallow, peanut-shaped candies and real peanuts in their shells.

Stu looked Pete up and down and said, "I like your cool outfit, Pete. "Isn't that your cape from Halloween? Are you gonna put on a lion taming show like we did when we made Luke's Lion Farm? It was cool to copy Gay's Lion Farm and their real lions that used to be in El Monte years ago."

Pete tipped back his black construction paper hat he made for our Fourth of July parade and answered, "Mary Jane ordered me to dance or stay seated. I am *not* to tame any lions! I told her I'd stay seated 'cause I don't dance . . . not square dance or waltz or any of that jazz."

"Believe me, you don't want to see me or Pete square dance," I said.

An appropriate song, "What Are You Doing New Year's Eve?" trilled from the record player. Our friends sang along while Pete drummed his fingers on the tabletop.

When that song ended, "See You Later, Alligator," by Bill Haley and His Comets, took its place. The teens jumped up from where they sat at tables around the dance floor and twirled to the beat of the tune.

The surfer boys, Cap, Ruler, Ten Man, and Full Bore, along with a gaggle of girls, mingled with Butch, Davey Boy, and The Cruiser's Car Club members. Mary Jane and Debbie swirled in their matching, iridescent snowflake outfits while Oliver and Nan danced together.

Pete said, "Tonight we're saying 'see ya later' to 1955. I'm waiting for one of the surfer dudes to yell 'surf's up' like they did last summer at the beach."

"Me too," I said. "Look how much fun Butch and The Cruisers are having on the dance floor. It's cool that the teens get along and do lots of California cruisin together."

"Earlier, when I walked across the street, I passed their cool cars parked out front," said Stu. "Butch's restored midnight-blue Merc, Ernie's '32 called Wild Panther, Cap's Woody, and Hawk's Ride are the best-looking machines in El Monte."

"In all of the state," said Pete. "Maybe even the nation." Pete pointed to the buffet table where Dan from Dan's Diner balanced a big box. "Hey, Dan's dropping off desserts from his diner's pie keeper. Yum."

"Oh, goodie," I said. "Your buffet bash dessert table covered in cookie creations reminds me of the bake sales we did to earn money for the Community Chest."

"That was a lot of work," said Edith, "but I was glad to help sell and . . . eat cookies."

"My mom still has baked goods in her freezer," said Eileen.

We laughed at our friends as the teens left the dance floor and crowded to the food tables. Tim led the way. With his braces hidden by his jeans, he stalked like a wooden soldier in that Christmas song about soldiers.

"Hey, look at Tim," said Pete. "Remember last spring when we sort of dipped into the mudhole and Tim told us how he got polio. We wanted him to walk without crutches so he wouldn't be the same as Mr. Chester."

Our heads swiveled to Mr. Chester's table where he sat with Adam's parents and Uncle Charlie's family. Little kids scampered around the table in their pajamas. Buddy bounced up then wagged his tail and head back and forth mimicking their actions.

"Last April first, Mr. Chester limped across his backyard using his crutch to move his crippled legs," I said. "His spiky gray hair, sticking up above our bush-covered fence, looked like my Granny Mary's mop."

"Yeah," said Pete. "We thought he was playing an April Fools' joke."

Susan said, "It's no joke that I like the circus art under this big top."

Becky pointed, "Look at that mural of the clowns in their costumes."

"The way that clown on the right is juggling those red balls reminds me of our Oak Glen gathering and the red apples that we juggled into our buckets," said Pete.

"It reminds me of the front yard fun we had when you dressed up as a clown pirate," I commented with a smile. "We chased the little kids around."

Pete raised his arms like he was flying and said, "I wanted to be Peter Pan Hawking but the little kids, dressed as Neverland characters, said 'no.'"

Stu said excitedly, "Remember the crocodile in the Peter Pan play that chased Captain Hook? It reminds me of the crocs and alligators at The California Alligator Farm. They crunched on stuff that sounded like . . . Buddy crunching dog biscuits." Buddy looked up holding a half-eaten treat in his teeth.

Our table erupted in laughter as Buddy dropped his treat and dipped his head sideways with one ear hanging down. Becky said, "I like that mural over there with the dancing dogs in front of those fancy-looking horses ridden by the pretty ballerinas."

Pete announced, "We didn't look so pretty when we rode horses in Lytle Creek Canyon or the burros at Knott's Berry Farm. We looked dusty."

Eileen said, "You and Carol Ann went to lots of cool places this year like the Arboretum, Christmas Tree Lane, and Santa's Village."

Bob Bailey said, "My folks took me and my brother to the mountains to play in the snow at Santa's Village a few weeks ago. It was cool."

"I think you mean cold," said Susan. "*Very cold.*"

"I feel really lucky I went to lots of great places this past year," I said, "like Huntington Beach, Los Angeles, Sturtevant Falls, ferocious football games, and downtown in the tank." *And every time I ended up back at my home sweet home.*

While the teens danced to more rock 'n' roll sounds, Stu said, "Pete, all year long, your family had the coolest parties in your backyard. I heard about Mary Jane's pink birthday bash and Hawk's Hawaiian luau where Buddy chased a cat and caused a scene."

"Then you moved into our neighborhood," said Pete. "And you got to go to Hawk's Harvest Party on Halloween dressed up like Moses with his Ten Commandments."

"Yeah, that was boss," said Stu. "So was Christmas in this tent."

"What's boss are the decorations for *all* the parties," I said.

"Yeah, and the good weather tonight," said Pete. "After suffering through a year of wacky weather including a dust devil on our school playground, smog, fog, rain, Santa Ana winds, stifling heat, a crazy cloudburst, and a Gravel Gertie flood, I'm happy to sit here in a cool and still tent under a cloudless, star-studded sky."

"Yeah, me too," said Bob Bailey as he nodded his head up and down.

"At least Mary Jane is having fun and leaving us alone," I said as I glanced at her on stage. "She spent the year of 1955 leaning, sitting, and stepping in smelly and unsavory stuff that sloshed, spilled, and smashed on her backside, head, or feet."

"Don't look now," said Pete, "but she did it again! She can't blame us for those orange marshmallow, peanut-shaped candies dangling from the back of her pink, puffy, sparkly skirt."

"Yikes," I said as I looked for a place to hide. "She'll blame us like she always does when she finds those sticky candies latched onto her skirt like orange leeches."

Just then, Debbie joined Mary Jane on stage and whispered in her ear. Pete's sister looked at the back of her costume and briskly brushed at her "attachments." Then she turned around and glared in our direction.

"Looks like there's trouble on stage," said Pete, "so let's quickly go visit the buffet." *Oops, we're in trouble again,* I thought.

We surged from our table like a wave on the seashore. Pajama-clad kids galloped by us. My beautiful aunt, Dr. Ruth McCammon, Pete's mom, and Adam's mom rushed to catch up with Mandy, my sisters, my cousins, and Adam's younger sister.

It looks like the moms are rounding up their children like a herd of circus ponies are rounded up when it's time to take them home to their . . . beds, I thought. Behind them, Tim's painted mural showcased a herd of pretty, prancing circus ponies.

Ahead of us in the food line, Hawk said to Tim, "I can't believe your good luck! You sold all your painted murals to a real circus that's using them for advertising. It was clever of you to paint the tent opening and circus animals on the backdrop from Carol Ann's play."

Tim acknowledged Hawk's compliment, glanced in my direction, then smiled as they moved forward in line to refill their food plates. When it was our turn, we piled hot dogs, chips, and baked beans on our plates.

While balancing his plate Pete said, "It's our last meal of 1955 and I'm gonna enjoy every bite. That's why I got a handful of Mrs. H's chocolate chip cookies 'cause they're the best in the west!"

"Nice rhyme," said Stu. "They taste and look a million times better than Mrs. Rose's Mincemeat Mold that she made for our class party."

Stu's remark raised exaggerated moans from our table. A rock 'n' roll tune blared from Mary Jane's record player. *Where is Pete's sister?* I scanned the stage then shrugged my shoulders at her disappearance.

"What are you looking for, Carol Ann?" asked a vicious voice next to my ear which caused me to sit up with a start. I turned *slowly* in my seat and *stared* into Mary Jane's squinty, mean-looking eyes. *Yikes!*

"Oh, nothing," I said with a shiver. "I was admiring your decorating skills. This circus is . . . Coolsville."

"Cut the compliments, Carol Ann," snarled Mary Jane. "My lovely, pink costume is covered in candy and it's . . . not your fault . . . for once." She laughed like a hyena.

Pete spoke up, "Thanks, Sis, for not blaming us for what looks like orange icicles hanging on your skirt." I looked down at Buddy and gave him "the look" so he wouldn't do any jumping up to chomp those orange marshmallow treats with his teeth.

"You're welcome. Happy New Year," she said then scurried away.

"What a close call," said Pete. "Maybe Sis is changing . . . or not."

As the hands on my watch neared midnight, "Rock Around the Clock," by Bill Haley and His Comets, soared over and around the teens as they dipped, swirled, and swayed. Our friends sitting nearby watched the action on the dance floor. I pulled my red, spiral-sided notepad and stubby pencil from the pocket in my party dress.

Pete looked at it and said, "You filled that notepad with cool stuff all year: clues, close calls, weather information, and boss Bible verses."

"This notepad was handy. I'm saving it and buying a new one for the New Year," I said. "I hope it's calmer than the wild winter we just had."

"I hope so," said Pete. "but I still want a New Year full of more cool and exciting adventures."

"I'm ready to welcome 1956 and its adventures," I said. "I hope it's not as scary, sinister, ferocious, or wild as 1955."

"Let's wait and see," said Pete with a grin on his face while holding a turning, twisting noisemaker in one hand and a chocolate chip cookie in the other. Whistles, horns, and Buddy's howling exploded like firecrackers on the Fourth of July throughout the circus tent on this very first day of January.

The song, "You'll Never Walk Alone," circled the circus of friends and family as we welcomed the New Year with cheers, whistles, whoops, hugs, yells, and smiling faces. Like a group of cool circus performers in their grand finale, we ushered out the old year and welcomed in the brand new one . . . 1956 . . . and all of its brand new adventures. *Yea!*

Carol Ann

Season's Greetings

FAMILY PHOTO

Ca...
on a...

A CHICAGO CHRISTMAS
Mom holding Kathleen

Cathie, Aunt Ruthie, Jimmie
Uncle Charlie, and Little C

Kathleen, Jimmie, Aun...
Pamela, Gail, Carol A...
and David in fro...
Aunt Ruth...

CHRISTMAS 1950
Carol Ann leaning on Kathleen

n talking
lephone

Dad
(Harry Hartnell)

CHRISTMAS

Carol Ann, Kathleen, Mark,
Dad, Mom and Gail

, Little Charlie,
dy Cathie,

lace

Gail with Santa Claus

DRESSED UP
Carol Ann in
Party Dress

COWGIRL
CHRISTMAS
Carol Ann models
her cowgirl outfit

Granny Catherine
and "Great" Aur

Gail, Carol Ann, Mark
and Kathleen

Wishing you a very *Merry Christmas*

Gail, Carol Ann and Kathleen

A CHICAGO CHRISTMAS

Dad holding Kathleen
with Christmas Tree
in background

FOR MORE INFORMATION

The Santa Claus Lane Parade
www.thesantaclauslaneparade.com

"Here Comes Santa Claus" song by Gene Autry
www.herecomessantaclaus.com

Santa's Village in Skyforest, California 1955-1998
www.santasvillageskyforest.com

Christmas Tree Lane in Altadena, California
www.christmastreelane.com

Balian Mansion/Christmas light display
www.balianmansion.com

Rosa Parks
www.rosaparks.com

Los Angeles County Hospital
www.losangelescountyhospital.com

El Monte Historical Society and Museum/Donna Crippen
3150 Tyler Avenue, El Monte, California 91731
www.elmontehistoricalsociety.com

El Monte Chamber of Commerce
10501 Valley Boulevard, El Monte, California 91734-1866
www.elmontechamberofcommerce.com

Rosemead Library, County of Los Angeles Public Library
8800 Valley Boulevard, Rosemead, California 91770-1788
El Monte Herald newspaper on microfilm
www.rosemeadlibrary.com

Hawk's Ride   1937 Ford
www.hawksride.com

Route 66 "Mother Road" Museum
681 N. First Avenue, Barstow, California 92311
(760) 255-1890   www.route66museum.org

California Route 66 Museum
16825 South D Street, Victorville, California 92393-2151
(760) 951-0436
www.califrt66museum.org

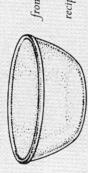

from the kitchen of _____Mrs. Jeanne Hartnell_____

recipe for _Christmas Cut-Out Cookies_

ingredients

½ cup butter softened
1 cup brown sugar
2 eggs
1 teaspoon vanilla extract

2 ½ cups all purpose flour
1 teaspoon baking powder
1 teaspoon salt
½ teaspoon ground cinnamon

instructions

Heat oven to 350 degrees. In large bowl mix together butter, sugar, eggs, and vanilla extract until blended. Add flour and baking powder, salt and cinnamon. Mix until blended. Chill dough in covered bowl for at least one hour in the refrigerator. Roll out dough on a floured board until 1/8 inch thick. Cut out desired shapes with 3 inch cookie cutters. Place shapes on ungreased cookie sheet and bake for 8 to 10 minutes until golden brown. Let cool on cookie sheet for 2 minutes then move cookies to wire racks or a brown paper bag to cool completely. Frost with Buttercream Icing and decorate with colorful candy sprinkles. Makes about 4 dozen cookies.

BUTTERCREAM ICING

2 cups confectioner's sugar   ¼ cup softened butter
2 tablespoons of milk   ½ teaspoon vanilla extract
Blend together until smooth. Frost cookies with icing. Shake candy sprinkles over the soft icing.

■ 141 ■

Glossary of 1950s Words

AFTER WHILE, CROCODILE: to say goodbye.

AGITATE THE GRAVEL: to leave/ to walk on the road.

ANKLE-BITER: a child.

APE or GO APE: to get really mad.

BAD NEWS: a depressing person/ someone who means trouble.

BASH: a great party.

BLAST: a good time.

BOSS: great.

BREAD: money

BUG: to bother someone.

BURN RUBBER: to accelerate very fast with a car.

CHERRY: an attractive-looking car.

CHROME-PLATED: a fancy car.

CLOUD 9: really happy or dreamy.

COOKIN: doing something well.

COOL: a long, drawn out word meaning someone or something extraordinary.

COOL IT: relax and settle down.

COOTIES: invisible infestations of the uncool.

CRUISIN' FOR A BRUISIN: looking for trouble.

CUT OUT: to leave.

DIBS: to stake a claim to something.

DIG: to approve or understand.

DIG IN: to eat food.

DREAMLAND: a place to sleep.

EYEBALL: look around.

FAT CITY: a great thing or place.

FIRE UP: start your engine.

FLAT OUT: to go as fast as you can.

FLICK: a movie.

FLOOR IT: put a car's gas pedal to the floor.

FRACTURE: to amuse.

FROSTED: angry.

GERMSVILLE: a place full of germs.

GET WITH IT: to understand something.

GIG: work or a job.

GOOF: someone who makes mistakes.

GOOPY/ GROTTY: messy/ dirty.

HANG OUT: to be someplace.

HEAT: the police.

HIP: cool/ with it/ in the know.

HOPPED UP: a car modified for speed.

HORN: telephone.

HOTTIE: a very fast car.

ILLUMINATIONS: good ideas/ good thoughts.

IN ORBIT: to know something.

JELLYROLL: a hairdo.

JETS: to have brains/ smarts.

KICK: a fun or good thing.

LATER GATOR or SEE YA LATER, ALLIGATOR: to say goodbye.

LIKE CRAZY, LIKE WOW: really good and better than cool.

MACHINE: a car.

MADE IN THE SHADE: success is guaranteed.

MAKE THE SCENE: to attend an event.

MOST: high praise of someone.

NEST: a hairdo.

NOD: drift off to sleep.

NO SWEAT: not a problem.

ODDBALL: someone not normal/ uncool.

PAD: home/ room.

PAPER SHAKER: a cheerleader.

PARTY POOPER: no fun at all.

PILE UP Z'S: to get some sleep.

POP THE CLUTCH: to release a car's clutch fast.

POUND: beat up.

PUNCH IT: step on the car's gas pedal to go fast.

PUT DOWN: to say bad things about someone.

RATTLE YOUR CAGE: to get really upset.

ROCK: a diamond.

ROCKET: a fast car.

SCOLDED US ROYALLY: to get in trouble.

SCREAM: to go fast.

SCREAMER: a fast car.

SHOT DOWN: failed.

SIDES: vinyl music records.

SING: to tattle.

SOUNDS: music.

SOUPED UP: a car modified to go fast.

SPLIT: to leave.

STORE BOUGHT: bought from the store.

TANK: a large car driven by parents.

THINK FAST: said right before something is thrown.

THREADS: clothes.

UNCOOL: opposite of cool and not good.

UNREAL: hard to believe.

WHAT'S BUZZIN CUZZIN?: a question about what's happening.

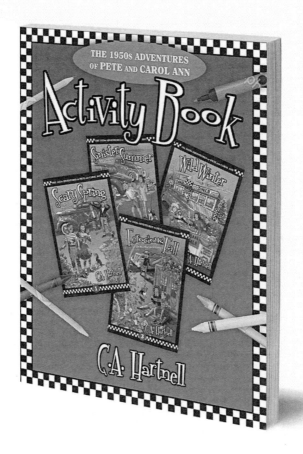

Follow the further adventures of Pete and Carol Ann
in their activity and coloring book.

Enjoy: coloring pages, mazes, word searches, dot to dot,
word scrambles, and many more fun activities.

Wild Winter Word Scramble

UNSCRAMBLE THE FOLLOWING WORDS

1) DERERINE   1) _ _ _ _ _ _ _ _

2) WNSO   2) _ _ _ _

3) ELJIGN LELBS   3) _ _ _ _ _ _   _ _ _ _ _

4) ASNTSA LGEALIV   4) _ _ _ _ _ _   _ _ _ _ _ _ _

5) LOCO TCAO   5) _ _ _ _   _ _ _ _

6) BLLSOWNA   6) _ _ _ _ _ _ _ _

7) GNRAERIDBGE   7) _ _ _ _ _ _ _ _ _ _ _

8) DYCNA NECA   8) _ _ _ _ _   _ _ _ _

9) TNROH LOPE   9) _ _ _ _ _   _ _ _ _

10) FLE   10) _ _ _

11) SCHISTMAR ETER   11) _ _ _ _ _ _ _ _ _   _ _ _ _

12) YSFRSOKTE   12) _ _ _ _ _ _ _ _ _

13) TANAS LAUCS   13) _ _ _ _ _   _ _ _ _ _

14) EPNI ETSRE   14) _ _ _ _   _ _ _ _ _

15) YOT HOSP   15) _ _ _   _ _ _ _

ANSWERS

1) REINDEER
2) SNOW
3) JINGLE BELLS
4) SANTAS VILLAGE
5) COOL COAT
6) SNOWBALL
7) GINGERBREAD
8) CANDY CANE
9) NORTH POLE
10) ELF
11) CHRISTMAS TREE
12) SKYFOREST
13) SANTA CLAUS
14) PINE TREES
15) TOY SHOP

How many words can you spell from

Wild Winter: Christmas, Clues, and Crooks

1) _____
2) _____
3) _____
4) _____
5) _____
6) _____
7) _____
8) _____
9) _____
10) _____
11) _____
12) _____
13) _____
14) _____
15) _____
16) _____
17) _____
18) _____
19) _____
20) _____
21) _____
22) _____
23) _____
24) _____
25) _____

26) _____
27) _____
28) _____
29) _____
30) _____
31) _____
32) _____
33) _____
34) _____
35) _____
36) _____
37) _____
38) _____
39) _____
40) _____
41) _____
42) _____
43) _____
44) _____
45) _____
46) _____
47) _____
48) _____
49) _____
50) _____

Nehemiah 8:10 "...the joy of the LORD is your strength!"

Color This Page

COVER CREATION

Collage of *Wild Winter* Cover by C.A. Hartnell

Rough Sketch of *Wild Winter* Cover

Artist, Larry Rupert, drew this rough sketch/line drawing
of the *Wild Winter* Cover

Final *Wild Winter* Cover

Larry colorized this final line drawing then it went to
a graphic artist for the final artistic touches.

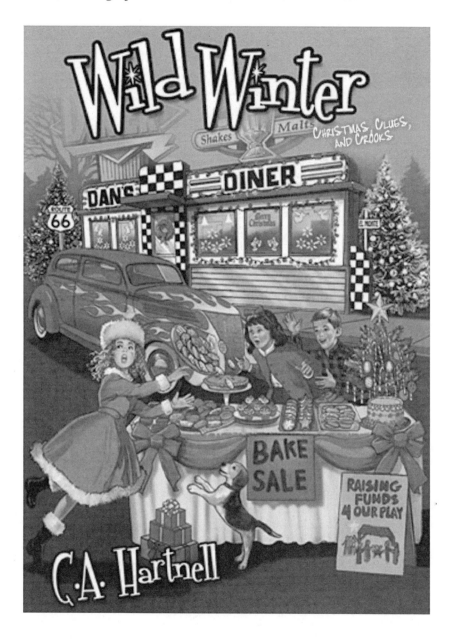

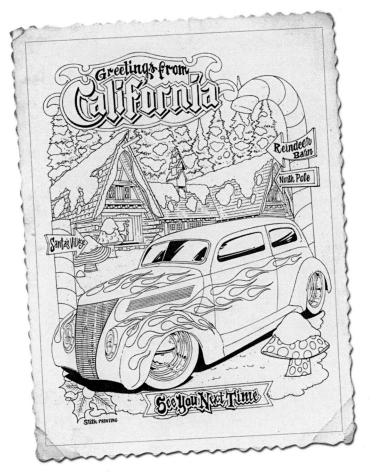

" . . . the joy of the LORD is my strength."

NEHEMIAH 8:10

Carol A. Hartnell and her husband live in the Southwest. They are blessed with four grown children and twelve grandchildren.
Visit the author at: www.cahartnell.com